The Cir
by Ba

Dynasties: The Danforths

An exciting new family saga!

A family of prominence…
tested by scandal, sustained by passion!

SAVANNAH SPECTATOR

A certain Savannah patriarch has announced his intention to run for the Senate, so his second oldest son might have to end his run as one of the city's most eligible bachelors. The hunky shipping tycoon was spotted with a petite and curvy beauty at a popular nightspot and they were generating enough steam to make those watching blush! Just who is the mystery woman?

Man Beneath the Uniform
by Maureen Child

SAVANNAH SPECTATOR

Sources say a certain reclusive Savannah heiress has a bodyguard. And not just any bodyguard, but a US Navy SEAL with a body worth keeping an eye on! The hunky baby-sitter and the black-haired beauty were seen on several moonlit walks, and even dancing quite intimately at a family soirée at one of Savannah's most gracious houses.

Apparently Daddy is worried about the safety of his only daughter. Could it be his senatorial campaign is ruffling more than a few feathers? And does the bodyguard's job include cosying up to one of the city's wealthiest young women? Is it duty, or love?

The Cinderella Scandal
BARBARA McCAULEY

Man Beneath the Uniformn
MAUREEN CHILD

SILHOUETTE®
Desire™

*Silhouette, Silhouette Desire and Colophon
are registered trademarks of Harlequin Books S.A.,
used under licence.*

*First published in Great Britain 2005
Silhouette Books, Eton House, 18-24 Paradise Road,
Richmond, Surrey TW9 1SR*

The publisher acknowledges the copyright holders of the
individual works as follows:

The Cinderella Scandal © Harlequin Books S.A. 2004
Man Beneath the Uniform © Harlequin Books S.A. 2004

*Special thanks and acknowledgement are given to Barbara McCauley
and Maureen Child for their contribution to the
Dynasties: The Danforths series.*

ISBN 0 373 60187 5

51-0105

*Printed and bound in Spain
by Litografia Rosés S.A., Barcelona*

THE CINDERELLA SCANDAL
by
Barbara McCauley

SILHOUETTE®

Desire™ 2 in 1

presents

DYNASTIES:
THE DANFORTHS

*A family of prominence...tested by scandal,
sustained by passion!*

Also look for DYNASTIES: SUMMER IN SAVANNAH
Barbara McCauley, Maureen Child and Sheri WhiteFeather
Available in June 2005

To my readers everywhere—thank you!
You are all special to me. I wish you much love,
laughter and happiness.

BARBARA McCAULEY,

who has written more than twenty novels for Silhouette
Books, lives in Southern California with her own hand-
some hero husband, Frank, who makes it easy to
believe in and write about the magic of romance.
Barbara's stories have won and been nominated for
numerous awards, including the prestigious RITA®
Award from the Romance Writers of America, Best
Desire of the Year from *Romantic Times* and Best
Short Contemporary from the National Reader's
Choice Awards.

Barbara loves to hear from her readers. Please e-mail
her at www.barbaramccauley.com

DYNASTIES: THE DANFORTHS

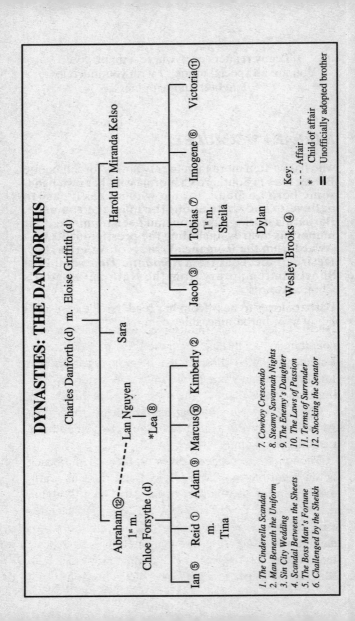

Charles Danforth (d) m. Eloise Griffith (d)

Abraham ⑫ - - - - - Lan Nguyen   Sara   Harold m. Miranda Kelso

1ˢᵗ m.
Chloe Forsythe (d)   *Lea ⑧

Ian ⑤   Reid ①   Adam ⑨   Marcus ⑩   Kimberly ②   Jacob ③   Tobias ⑦   Imogene ⑥   Victoria⑪

m.   1ˢᵗ m.
Tina   Sheila

                    Wesley Brooks ④   Dylan

1. The Cinderella Scandal
2. Man Beneath the Uniform
3. Sin City Wedding
4. Scandal Between the Sheets
5. The Boss Man's Fortune
6. Challenged by the Sheikh

7. Cowboy Crescendo
8. Steamy Savannah Nights
9. The Enemy's Daughter
10. The Laws of Passion
11. Terms of Surrender
12. Shocking the Senator

Key:
- - - Affair
* Child of affair
== Unofficially adopted brother

One

Sheets of icy January rain rippled across the Savannah countryside. Lightning exploded in the dark sky. Thunder rumbled through the magnificent oaks that lined the private stone drive, rattled the wide, sweeping branches and shook the moss-covered trunks.

The night wasn't fit for man nor beast, but when Abraham Danforth called his family to gather for a meeting, they came.

Though white-capped waves crashed on the beach below Crofthaven Manor, Reid Danforth was warm and dry inside the comfort of his car. Duke Ellington drifted quietly from the BMW's CD player, blended with the sound of the pelting rain on the car's roof and the *whish-whish* of the windshield wipers. After a long, hectic day negotiating a shipping contract with Maximilian Paper Products, one of Danforth & Co.'s largest clients in Austria, Reid was grateful for the peaceful thirty-minute drive to his family's house.

A drive, Reid thought as he pulled in front of the tall, black wrought-iron gates, that was about to come to an end.

Releasing a long breath, Reid pressed the remote inside his car, watched the massive gates slowly part. A flash of lightning lit the huge Georgian-style mansion at the end of the driveway; thunder boomed like cannon fire. Light shone through large, leaded-glass windows. Even to Reid, who'd been raised here in between semesters away at boarding schools, Crofthaven was an impressive estate. Built in the 1890s by Reid's great-grandfather, Hiram, the large mansion had been designed to survive. A trait Hiram had also firmly ingrained in his descendants.

Reid parked between two of the family's three limousines and shut off his engine, sat for a moment and listened to the rain battering the roof of his car. It always took a few moments to make the transition between the real world and Crofthaven. Tonight his father would expect the entire Danforth clan to be attentive while he laid out the game plan for his upcoming senatorial bid. Family unity and support were critical to a successful campaign. Abraham Danforth did not know the meaning of failure, a fact that had made the already prosperous shipping magnate more wealthy than his forefathers. Wealthy enough to step away from the day-to-day operations of Danforth & Co. Shipping and launch a new career in politics.

Because he was already late, Reid stepped out of his car into the piercing rain and strode toward the front entry. When he opened the oversize oak door, a gust of wind whistled around him, then swirled inside the white marbled hall. On a table at the base of the majestic sweeping staircase sat a large crystal vase filled with white roses that scented the air, as did the heavenly smell of roast lamb and oregano.

"Master Reid." Joyce Jones, Crofthaven's head housekeeper, appeared suddenly. Concern narrowed her brown eyes as she moved toward him. "I was worried about you."

"I'm fine," Reid reassured the woman he'd known the entire thirty-two years of his life. "Just finishing up some paperwork at the office."

Though the sixty-something housekeeper had never been especially demonstrative or affectionate, she at least had been a constant in Reid's erratic upbringing. The same black uniform, the same sturdy work shoes. Even the simple knot of brown hair at the base of her head hadn't changed, though lately Reid had noticed more than a few gray strands.

"It's nasty out there." Joyce moved behind Reid to help him out of his damp trench coat. Out of habit, she brushed a hand over the shoulders of his black business suit, then straightened the back of his collar. "Martin is serving spiced rum and martinis in the parlor. Your father's on a phone call in his office. I'll tell him you're here."

"Thanks."

Loosening his tie, Reid made his way to the parlor, then paused in the doorway. Two of his brothers, Ian and Adam were huddled by the fireplace with his cousin Jake, no doubt discussing the chain of D&D's

coffeehouses they'd started in the Savannah area. Beside the bar, Reid's youngest brother, Marcus—the lawyer in the family—was currently engaged in an intense legal discussion with their uncle Harold and cousin Toby, something about water rights on Toby's ranch in Wyoming.

Reid thought of his mother and wished she could be here now to see how her five children had grown. Though he'd only been eight when she'd died, he could still remember how she'd enjoyed cooking for the family, and how much she'd loved to throw parties here. Many a time he and Ian had sneaked downstairs and watched while all the beautiful people in their beautiful clothes laughed and ate and danced to a band. He would never forget the night of his mother's birthday party when Reid watched his father dancing with his wife under the silvery light of the ballroom chandelier.

She'd died the next week, and Abraham Danforth had never seemed the same since. None of them had been the same.

"Reid!" His sister Kimberly broke away from the conversation she'd been having with their cousin Imogene. "Look at you. You're all wet."

"I've been telling him that for years," Jake said from across the room as he lifted his martini glass in a toast. "The gang's all here."

"Where's Aunt Miranda?" Reid asked Kimberly as she rose on her tiptoes and kissed his cheek.

"Putting Dylan to bed upstairs." Kimberly smiled at the mention of Toby's three-year-old son. "I brought a scrapbook of fish I've been photographing and studying out at the island, and he wanted to look at them in lieu of a bedtime story.''

''Better watch out or we'll have another marine biologist in the family,'' Reid teased.

''If you'd have been here earlier and heard him playing the piano, you'd change your mind about that,'' Kimberly said. ''He'll be in Carnegie Hall by the time he's ten.''

''My money says he'll be there by eight.'' Imogene placed a vodka martini in Reid's hand. ''Hello, cuz.''

''Ah, the proud aunt.'' Reid grinned at Imogene, then leaned forward and kissed her cheek. ''How's the world of investment banking these days?''

''Two promotions in six months. Your tie's crooked.'' She tightened the knot he'd just loosened. ''Impression is everything, hon. Speaking of, where's Mitzi these days? You two are quite the handsome couple.''

''I have no idea where she is,'' he said dryly. ''Shopping, most likely.''

He hadn't seen Mitzi Birmingham in more than four months, thank the good Lord. For that matter, he'd been so busy at work putting things in order so he could take the next few weeks off and set up a campaign headquarters for his father, Reid hadn't been dating anyone. Which was just fine with him. When it came to women, he seemed to be a magnet for every money-hungry, status-seeking female in Savannah. As soon as a woman found out he was the son of Abraham Danforth, that he was the director of Danforth & Co. Shipping and that he lived in a penthouse, they either smothered him with compliments and giggled at everything he said or played coy games. Or worse, they did all three.

He knew that the lack of a warm, willing female in his bed would catch up with him soon, but for the moment, at least, he was content to concentrate on his work.

"Reid."

At the sound of his father's deep voice, Reid turned. Nicola Granville, Abraham's new campaign manager, stood by his side. "Dad. Miss Granville."

"Nicola, please. Nice to see you again, Reid."

Reid had met the tall redhead once at his father's office in town and spoken with her twice on the phone. At thirty-seven the woman had already made quite a name for herself in image consulting and politics, and Reid thought his father had made the right choice by hiring her. She was attractive, confident and hard-working. His father and Nicola would make quite a formidable team.

"Nice of you to join us," Abraham said evenly.

Though there hadn't been the slightest hint of irritation in his tone, Reid knew his father well enough to recognize a reprimand when he heard one. Reid also knew better than to offer excuses.

At fifty-five, Abraham Danforth had seasoned into a politician's dream. With his thick, dark-brown hair, deep blue eyes, broad shoulders and the famous Danforth smile, Reid had no doubt that his father would win the upcoming election, especially under the "Honest Abe" campaign slogan that Nicola had worked up.

"Everyone." Abraham's voice stilled the ongoing

conversations in the room. "For those of you who haven't met her already, I'd like to introduce my new campaign manager, Nicola Granville. After dinner she'll be outlining the upcoming campaign and family protocol."

While Nicola circulated around the room and met the family, Reid made his way over to his cousin Jake. "Where's Wes?"

"On a business trip." Jake lifted a brow. "Or so he says. You know Wes."

Reid smiled. Wes had been Jake's roommate in college, but the Danforths all thought of Wesley Brooks as one of the family. Despite Wes's reputation as a playboy, Reid knew that he would have been here if it had been possible.

Jake snagged a cracker with cheese as Martin passed by with a tray. "I heard you've found a building on Drayton to rent for campaign headquarters."

"Just the bottom floor," Reid said, sipping his martini. "I've spoken to the owner, Ivan Alexander, but I haven't signed anything yet. I'll meet with him tomorrow and take a look at the inside. He also owns the building and business next door, Castle Bakery."

Jake nodded. "They've got a good reputation. I've been meaning to get down there myself and check it out. We're always looking for new items on the menu at D&D's." Jake leaned in and wiggled one eyebrow. "And I've also heard that Ivan's got three daughters that look tasty, too."

"Since you're looking for some 'new items,'" Reid said with a grin, "maybe you should handle setting up the campaign headquarters."

"And deprive you of all the fun?" Jake dropped a hand on Reid's shoulder. "I wouldn't dream of it."

Before Reid could reply, Joyce announced that dinner was ready. As the family made their way to the dining room, the conversation turned to campaign strategies and procedures. The election was barely one year away, and Reid knew that the next twelve months were going to be busy. No doubt, there would be obstacles along the way, some predicted, some unseen. The entire Danforth family would be challenged, collectively and individually. Reid knew that he needed to stay focused and on track if he was going to help his father become a United States senator.

The last thing he had time for, Reid thought, no matter how "tasty," they might be, was Ivan Alexander's daughters.

With a sigh, Reid took his place at the table with the rest of his family and knew it was going to be a very long year.

Tina Alexander loved days when the chaos she called her life ran smoothly. The days when she didn't burn a single loaf of bread or an entire tray of apple Danish. The days when all the employees scheduled to work at her family's bakery actually showed up. The days when her sister Sophia wasn't having a man crisis and even managed to make her afternoon shift on time. The days that her other sister Rachel didn't lock herself in the back office and hide behind computer ledgers and sales accounts.

Tina especially enjoyed the rare days her mother

wasn't busy meddling in all three of her daughters' lives.

Today, however, was not one of those days.

"Sophia went to one of those dancing clubs again last night." Mariska Alexander gave a disapproving sniff while she boxed up a phone order for two dozen chocolate cupcakes. Mariska, with her aristocratic nose, strong European jaw and thick blond hair she always wore in a French twist, was definitely the queen of Castle Bakery.

"She did not come home until two in the morning," Mariska continued, even though Tina gave her mother no encouragement to do so. "Two o'clock! Without so much as a phone call."

Tina taped the lid shut on the box of Danish she'd just filled. The morning had been hectic, with only herself and their counter manager, Jason, working up front. There were customers to help, orders to fill and display cases to replenish before the noon rush hit. The last thing Tina needed right now was to listen to her mother lament her oldest daughter's transgressions.

"You placed an ad in the paper for a counter clerk," Tina said in an attempt to divert her mother's attention, then nodded at two young men sitting at a table in the corner of the bakery. The one with black spiked hair and ragged jeans appeared bored, while the one wearing a short-sleeved shirt and black slacks was reading a book. "Are you going to interview them?"

As if she hadn't even heard Tina's question, Mariska pointed to her face. "Look at my eyes. They are bloodshot from waiting up for your sister."

Tina sighed silently and slid the box of Danish

across the counter to Beverly Somersworth, the customer Tina had been helping. Like the majority of Castle Bakery customers, Beverly worked in the downtown Savannah business district. Every Thursday the plump, sixty-year-old brunette bought one dozen Danish for the legal office where she worked as a receptionist.

"Sophia is twenty-eight years old, Mom," Tina said as patiently as she could manage. "You don't need to wait up for her."

"My daughter is out until all hours of the night." Mariska shifted her attention to Beverly. "How could I sleep?"

"Eight or twenty-eight, a mother worries about her children," Beverly agreed as she fished around her purse for her wallet. "More than one night, I remember pacing my living room until my Eleanor came home. Thank goodness she finally got married and settled down. Have I shown you pictures of my grandchildren?"

Only ten times, Tina wanted to say, but she didn't, of course. She simply smiled and nodded when Beverly whipped the pictures out with the speed of a policeman flashing a badge.

"Ah, so lucky you are." Mariska sighed with envy. "I fear I will never be a grandmother. Sophia is dating too many young men, Rachel spends all her time at the movies and museums, and my Tina—" Mariska tweaked Tina's cheek "—she is just a baby herself."

I'm twenty-four, for God's sake, Tina thought and gritted her teeth. Because she was the youngest, she knew her mother saw her as the baby and, no matter what her age, probably always would. But she supposed it made no difference, anyway. Tina knew she could never accept a proposal.

Any man who would actually *want* to marry into the Alexander family couldn't possibly be right in the head.

Not that she didn't love her family. Her two sisters, mother, father and Aunt Yana were the only family she had. She loved them with all her heart.

But they were all just so...overwhelming. Her father looked and acted more like he was in collections for a loan shark than a baker. With just a look, Ivan Alexander had scared off every man who'd come to date his daughters. The ones who'd managed to survive Ivan never made it past Mariska, who asked endless questions regarding their job status, their family lineage and the question that really sent them running—did they like children?

Tina figured the only way she'd ever be able to marry was if she were witness to a mob murder and testified, then put under the witness protection program. Then, by some miracle, if she found Mr. Right, he would never be able to meet her family.

A little extreme, but it just might work.

Tina helped the next customer while her mother continued to ooh and aah over the baby pictures. When Beverly finally left, Mariska slipped off her apron and reached for her purse.

"The chamber of commerce has ordered twelve dozen muffins and ten dozen Danish for a breakfast tomorrow," Mariska said, pulling her sweater out from under the counter. "I have to run to the market for pecans and blueberries."

Tina glanced at the two young men sitting at the corner table. "But you were supposed to interview the applicants."

"Be a good girl and do that for me, dear." Mariska patted Tina's cheek.

"But—"

"Oh, and we need you to come in early tomorrow," Mariska said. "We have a heavy load of orders in the morning. Your father and I could use your help."

It wasn't a question, so Tina didn't bother to answer.

"I will be back shortly." With a quick wave Mariska disappeared down the hallway leading to the offices and back exit.

Tina stared after her mother, then sighed. It wasn't as if it was a problem to come in to work early. The most exciting thing going on in her life this evening was apartment-sitting for her aunt Yana while she was out of town for the next three weeks. Tina's hot date for the night was a cat and a video copy of *Sleepless in Seattle*.

"Sorry I'm late, T." Sophia breezed through the front entrance of the bakery. "I stopped to gas my car and darn if I didn't break a nail, so I just had to run by and see my manicurist."

The two applicants took one look at Sophia dressed in her black leather skirt, low-cut sweater and tall boots, and they snapped to attention. Sophia, who'd just recently put highlights in her already-blond hair, smiled at the young men. They puffed their chests out and sucked their guts in.

Tina frowned at her sister when she came behind the counter and reached for a black apron. "Must you torture every male you see?"

"I'm the one in torture," Sophia said smoothly. "So many men, so little time."

Tina rolled her eyes at her sister's foolishness. They were all so different. Sophia, the gorgeous green-eyed, blond man-eater; Rachel, the pretty, though timid, hazel-eyed brunette.

And then there's me, Tina thought.

Not blond like her mother, not dark like her father, but with her sandy-brown hair and light-brown eyes, somewhere in the middle, a mix of them both. She was the smart daughter, the level-headed daughter and—the label that Tina hated the most—the responsible daughter.

But what she really hated was the fact that it was true.

There was a crash from the kitchen, followed by a mumbled string of Hungarian curses. Sophia gnawed on her shiny, red bottom lip. "Ah, I'll be right back. I've got to go ask Rachel something about, ah, reimbursement for petty cash."

"Chicken," Tina said, but Sophia merely clucked as she hurried away.

Walking into her father's kitchen when he was in a foul mood was like entering a lion's den. You never knew if you'd come out alive.

With a lull in the storm, Tina knew she'd have to hurry and do the interviews before the lunch crowd flowed in. Slipping out of her black apron, she looked at Jason, who was ringing up an order for a cappuccino and a chocolate muffin.

The twenty-six-year-old counter clerk had a boyish charm about him: unruly dark-blond hair, deep-blue eyes, a lean, athletic build. Teenage girls and young women had a tendency to giggle and bat their eyelashes when he waited on them, and even older women seemed flustered by the counter clerk's good looks.

But Jason, much to Tina's distress, had eyes for only one woman.

With a sigh, Tina forced her mind back on business and asked the applicant with the spiked hair to follow her down the hall to her father's office.

The sidewalks in front of the narrow, three-story red-brick building were damp from the previous night's rain. Over the wide, bevelled-glass storefront window, drops of water still clung to the forest-green awnings.

Reid stared past the For Lease sign and scanned the empty office space. The location and square footage were exactly what he'd been looking for, and the rent was in the ballpark. Public parking two doors down and heavy traffic only sweetened the deal.

And speaking of sweet—Reid glanced at the building next door. The most incredible smells were coming from Ivan Alexander's bakery.

Based on the number of customers Reid had watched coming and going in the past few minutes, the business was doing very well. Housing his father's campaign headquarters next to the busy bakery would not only bring a lot of foot traffic, the staff and volunteers working the campaign would have easy access to food and drink.

By the end of the day Reid intended to have a lease signed and a key in his hand.

An overhead bell tinkled when he opened the oak-framed, bevelled-glass door of Castle Bakery. The scent of warm cinnamon, rich chocolate and freshly baked bread assaulted his senses. Reid glanced at the polished display cases of neatly stacked cookies, fancy cakes and assorted fruit pastries. His mouth literally watered. The place had an old world feel to it, he thought as he closed the door behind him. Stone floor, suit of armor in the corner, framed pictures of famous castles in Europe. Glass-topped tables with wrought-iron chairs allowed seating for customers, though currently only two of the tables were occupied: a man drinking a cup of coffee and munching on a muffin while he talked on his cell phone and a teenage boy reading a physics book.

Reid approached the counter and stood behind an elderly couple who couldn't make up their minds between prune Danish or apple tarts.

"Excuse me." Reid caught the counter clerk's attention. "I'm here about Mr. Alexander's ad for—"

"In the office—" the clerk raised a thumb toward a hallway "—third door on the left, across from Merlin."

Merlin? Reid followed the direction in which he'd been pointed and rounded the corner, then came face-to-face with a life-size statue of King Arthur's magician. Wand in hand, dressed in deep-blue velvet and wizard's hat, the whimsical, white-bearded figure greeted customers on their way to the rest rooms. Reid studied the realistic figure for a moment, then knocked on the office door.

"I'll be right with you."

The voice was distinctly female, Reid noted, and had a smooth, smoky quality. Fantasies, immediate and extremely erotic, pinballed in his brain. Reid hoped it wasn't Mrs. Alexander; he sure as hell didn't want to have the kind of thoughts he was having over another man's wife. Still, he couldn't wait to see if the voice matched the face.

Merlin seemed to glare at him.

"I'm only human," Reid said with a shrug, then folded his arms and leaned against the wall.

The door opened a moment later and a young man dressed in ragged jeans and a blue T-shirt that read, No Flash Photography, came out of the office.

"Hours suck," the guy muttered.

Lifting a brow, Reid watched him walk away, then turned back to the still-open door and stuck his head inside. A woman wearing a long-sleeved white blouse sat bent over a small, cluttered metal desk. Her sandy-brown ponytail cascaded down her long neck and skimmed one narrow shoulder. She held a pen between slender fingers while she made notes on a piece of paper.

"I was looking for—"

"One second." Her gaze still on her scribbling, she waved him in. "Would you mind closing the door, please?" Reid moved into the office and shut the door behind him. Because he couldn't quite see the woman's face, he studied her hands. Smooth skin. Nails short and neat. No polish, no rings.

"Before I have you fill out an application," she said without looking up, "I'd like to ask you—"

That's when her gaze lifted.

With the large-framed eyeglasses she wore, Reid might not have said that the woman was beautiful, but she was definitely pretty. Her skin was porcelain smooth over high cheekbones, her eyes wide and expressive, the color of smooth whiskey. Her lips, parted in midsentence, turned up slightly at the corners.

"—a few questions," she finished after a moment's hesitation.

Though it was brief, Reid saw the unshielded surprise in the woman's eyes, heard the breathless edge to her voice.

Just as quickly the moment was gone.

"I'm Tina Alexander." She straightened her shoulders and held out her hand. "Thank you for coming."

Tina's heart lurched when the man's large hand enclosed her own, and she struggled to hold on to her composure. She'd interviewed dozens of applicants before, but never one who looked quite like this.

And certainly none who'd made her brain cells turn to dust.

He was just over six foot, she assessed, and from what she could tell by the jeans, black crewneck sweater and denim jacket he wore, he was lean and muscular. *Handsome* was too easy a word to describe him, Tina thought. With his dark hair and good looks, he was more complicated than that simple word. Eyes so deep blue, so intense, that they had quite literally stolen her breath. Add to that a square jaw, a strong slash of brow and a firm mouth, and he had her pulse skipping.

Of course, the fact that her fingers were still enclosed in his wasn't helping, either.

She pulled her hand away and gestured to a chair on the other side of the desk. Though she was absolutely certain she'd never met this man before, he looked strangely familiar.

She shook the thought off. No matter. She couldn't possibly hire him, anyway. He would be too big a distraction for Sophia and, if she were going to be completely honest, for herself, as well.

But she could hardly tell him that, of course. Better to let him decide the position wouldn't be right for him. She'd start with a few basic questions, then discourage him with a job description.

"So, Mr.—" She hesitated, realizing she hadn't asked him his name.

"Reid Danforth," he finished for her. "Reid will be fine."

The name was familiar, too, she thought, but she couldn't place it. She wrote his name on the top line of the application.

"Reid." She pushed her glasses up with her index finger. "Do you have any problems getting to work on time or working early morning hours?"

Confusion furrowed his brow, and it took him a beat to answer. "Not usually."

"Do you have any medical conditions that prohibit you from lifting or doing physical labor?"

He narrowed his eyes. "No."

She made a note on the application that he was in good physical condition. As if she hadn't already noticed. Darn it, though. She'd been hoping for an easy way out.

She moved on to the next question. "Do you have any experience working in sales or with a cash register?"

He stared at her for a long moment, then one corner of his mouth slowly turned upward. It was really quite annoying what that casual half smile did to her stomach.

"I have some experience in sales," he said with a nod. "I've never worked a cash register, but I'm a fast learner."

I'm sure you are, Tina nearly said out loud. She also had no doubt that he would be quite good at sales. Lord knew she'd certainly want to buy something from him.

They hadn't talked about wages, she realized. Though the job was good pocket money for a teenager or college student, it was hardly enough for a more mature man to live on. "Is the hourly wage we advertised acceptable?"

To her discomfort, he leaned forward and leveled his gaze with hers. She caught the faint, spicy scent of his aftershave, and could hear her pulse beating in her ears.

"Let me just ask you this," he said, his voice smooth and deep and edged with amusement, "if I said the wage was irrelevant, would you hire me?"

Her first instinct was to say yes, but Tina knew it

would be wasting her time and his to give him false hope or continue this interview. "No."

"Why not?"

"Because—" she hesitated "—for one thing, you're...a little older than most of our applicants."

Irritation narrowed his eyes. "I'm too old for you?"

"Of course you're not too old for me," she said, then quickly tried to sidestep. "I mean, you're not too old." Oh, hell. She'd certainly gotten herself into a corner on this. There were laws against age discrimination. "It's just that we mostly hire teenagers and college students, that's all."

"You wouldn't hire me because I'm not a teenager or college student." He crossed his arms and looked down his nose at her. "So what else is wrong with me?"

"It's not that there's anything wrong with you." She chewed on her bottom lip. "Exactly."

He lifted a brow. "Exactly?"

"Well, there's also my sister, Sophia."

"What about her?"

"She is easily—" Tina searched for the right word "—distracted by good-looking men and vice versa."

"So you think I'm too old and too good-looking," he said dryly. "What else?"

When he repeated it all back, Tina knew it sounded absurd. She cursed herself for not having had him just fill out an application and leave. "You're overqualified."

"How do you know that?"

"You're obviously educated," she said. "You

speak well, exude confidence, and you look like you just stepped off the cover of *Fortune 500* or—''

It felt as if a lightbulb had flashed on.

Danforth. Of the Savannah Danforths. Shipping magnates. Big estate. Lots and lots of money. There'd been rumors that Abraham Danforth would be running for the Senate.

Everyone who lived in Savannah, and most everyone who didn't, had heard of the Danforth family.

Unable to speak, Tina continued to stare at Reid. That's why he looked so familiar. He *had* been on the cover of a magazine, *Savannah Business*. The issue Reid's face was on had been sitting in the customer magazine rack of the bakery for the past three months.

''You—'' her voice was a ragged whisper ''—you're...Abraham Danforth's...''

''Son,'' he finished for her, and stuck out his hand again. ''Reid Danforth. I'm here to rent the building next door.''

Two

Reid let the words hang between them while the woman digested her mistake. Her eyes had widened behind her glasses, and her cheeks bloomed a pretty shade of pink. She hadn't even released the breath she'd inhaled when she'd realized who he was.

He supposed he could make the situation easier by simply shrugging it off and assuring her there was no harm done. A simple misunderstanding. No big deal at all. It would certainly be the gentlemanly thing to do.

But, hell, it wouldn't be nearly as much fun.

He decided he would enjoy watching her squirm for a minute or two. Something told him that Tina Alexander was used to being composed and in control, and he rather liked the idea of ruffling this woman's feathers.

Especially after the crack about him being old. Dammit, thirty-two was not old!

But when she continued to stare at him with alarm in her eyes, he began to feel a little guilty. He just wanted to rattle her a bit, not humiliate her.

He opened his mouth with the intention of easing her embarrassment, but when the breath she'd been holding came rushing out like an icy snowstorm, he realized it wasn't embarrassment on her cheeks but annoyance.

"You knew perfectly well I was interviewing you for a job," she said tightly. "Why didn't you stop me?"

Well, well, he thought, raising a brow. The kitten definitely had her back up now.

"I suppose it was like watching a train wreck," he said with a half grin. "I just couldn't seem to tear myself away."

It was also refreshing not to be recognized, he realized. He'd always hated that people treated him differently when they knew he was a Danforth, either turned extremely helpful or absurdly friendly.

Though at this moment *friendly* would hardly be a word to describe Tina Alexander, Reid thought. The mouth he'd thought so soft only a moment ago now pressed into a thin line.

He wondered for one insane moment what those lips would feel like under his own.

"I'm glad I've given you a few minutes of entertainment." She crumpled the application under her fingers into a ball and tossed it into a trash can beside the desk. "Since you're obviously not here looking for a job, is there something else I can do for you?"

Well now, *that* was a leading question, Reid thought, but certainly not one he could honestly answer without getting thrown out of the office. "I'm here about the space next door."

She glanced up sharply. "What about it?"

"My real estate broker spoke to a man named Ivan Alexander about leasing it."

"Ivan is my father." Tina's eyes narrowed cautiously. "But there must be some mistake. That space isn't for lease."

"That's odd, since I was told to stop by today so I can look at the inside and pick up a key."

"But—" Her voice faltered, broke. "That can't be."

"I've already put a deposit down, Miss Alexander."

"A deposit?" she repeated, her cool tone now one of disbelief.

"My broker gave your father a check yesterday." Reid couldn't help but wonder why it should matter to Tina one way or the other who rented the space. "Is there a problem?"

Is there a problem? Tina stared at the man sitting across from her, felt a bubble of hysteria lodge in her throat. This can't be, she told herself. Surely her parents would have told her if they'd rented the space.

Her space.

But it was true. She knew it in her heart. Reid Danforth would not be sitting here if it weren't.

Slowly she slipped her reading glasses off, then

spread her hands on the desk and rose. "Will you excuse me a minute?"

Without waiting for him to answer, Tina walked stiffly from the room, then headed directly for the double doors of the kitchen entrance. Her father was bent over a work table, frosting the bottom layer of what was going to be a three-tier, whipped cream, strawberry shortcake.

Hands on her hips, she faced him. "How could you do this?"

"Very easy," he said without glancing up. "Slice the strawberries very thin and just the right amount of gelatine in the whip cream. Perfect every time."

"That's not what I mean and you know it." She snatched up the bowl of whipped cream sitting on the counter and held it away from him. "When the antique store moved out next door, you promised to rent the space to me."

"I make no promise." Frowning, he straightened and faced her, then folded his beefy arms over his wide chest. "I told you I think about it."

"It's a perfect spot for a sandwich and coffeehouse." She struggled to control her voice and her temper. "I poured my heart and soul into that project. Design plans for the interior, a prospectus, potential menus. You told me you were impressed."

He nodded. "I was."

"Then why?" Her voice trembled as she hugged the cold metal bowl close. "Why would you do this to me?"

"You are too young to open your own business,

Katina." His voice softened a bit. "When you are older, we will talk."

"Stop treating me like a child. I'm twenty-four," she said through clenched teeth. "Me, Rachel, Sophia. We *are* older. Why can't you see that?"

"I am your *apa*," Ivan said firmly. "It is my duty to take care of my family. We have only each other."

"Dad." She struggled against tears. "*Apa.* I've worked in this bakery with you since I was ten. You know I can do it."

"It is too much money."

"Aunt Yana is going to help—"

"This is not Yana's decision." Ivan's voice rose. "My sister has the blood of the gypsies, running from city to city, country to country. What does she know about business and responsibility?"

"She's dedicated to her work," Tina defended her aunt. "Just because she travels doesn't mean that—"

"Enough!" He lifted a hand to silence her. "It is done. I have rented the space for one year. We will talk again then."

"But—"

"Be a good girl, Katina." Ivan patted Tina on her head. "Now you will take Mr. Danforth next door and show him what he has paid for."

"What?" Her mouth dropped open. "You expect me—"

"You will do as I say." He snatched the bowl of whipped cream from her arms. "And you will be nice to this man. Do you understand?"

Tina opened her mouth to protest, then closed it again. She knew it was useless to argue at this point.

The deal with the Danforths had obviously been made. It was too late to change that, and if she pushed her father too far, he would never rent her the space.

And now she was supposed to be nice?

Setting her teeth, she marched back to the office. Outside the door she paused, then drew in a long, slow, calming breath. She'd already made a big enough fool of herself in front of Reid Danforth. She refused to add pathetic to his opinion of her, as well.

Certain her face might crack under the strain, she forced a smile and opened the door.

"Well," she said, breezing into the room and plucking a key from a hook beside the door. "It appears there was a wrinkle in our line of communication here, Mr. Danforth. When do you plan on moving in?"

"Tomorrow."

In spite of her determination to be calm, Tina felt her jaw go slack. "Tomorrow?"

"We're announcing my father's candidacy in a few days," he explained. "It's taken quite a while to find a space that meets our requirements, so I have to move quickly."

"I see." Regaining her composure, she nodded. "Well, shall we go have a look, then?"

The woman had certainly come back with a different attitude, Reid thought as he followed Tina into the hallway. She'd gone from Miss Tempest to Miss Hospitality in the space of about five minutes.

Not that he was buying her facade of serenity. Reid could see just a trace of tension in her eyes, hear the edge of stress in her silky-smooth voice. Under the surface of all that so-called calm, a storm was brewing.

No doubt about it, she intrigued him. Made him wonder what all that pent-up energy would be like in bed.

They stepped out the back door of the bakery into a lovely garden framed by high walls of aged brick and stucco. Lush ferns and plants surrounded stone benches, statues of smiling cherubs and a small rock pond.

"There's a private alley between the buildings," she said as they walked across the patio, her tone clipped and matter-of-fact.

She opened an iron gate and they stepped into the alley. Reid noted the wrought-iron stairs leading to the second and third levels above the space he'd rented. "Are the upper levels rented out?" he asked.

"My aunt's apartment is on the second floor and she has a photography studio on the third." They moved past the alley, stepped through a second gate into another garden. "She's traveling most of the time on shoots, if you're worried about her disturbing you."

As Reid followed Tina through the second garden to the back entrance of the building, he couldn't help but notice the sway of her slender hips and the fact that she had nice legs. Something told him that it wouldn't be Tina's aunt who would be disturbing him, he thought.

He forced his attention back to Tina, realized he'd missed part of what she'd been saying, something about the buildings being built in the early 1800s, then renovated in the 1970s.

Over the next year, there'd be numerous receptions

for donors and volunteers, Reid knew. For the smaller, more private gatherings, the brick patio, with its stone benches and two-tiered fountain, would be perfect. "Will I have use of the garden area?"

"Of course."

She moved to the bevelled-glass back door of the building and inserted the key into the lock. He watched her visibly square her shoulders and draw in a breath as she turned the knob.

The smell of fresh paint filled the cool and damp air inside the wide hallway they stepped into; Reid realized that the layout was very similar to the bakery's. The afternoon sun spilled in through the back door and glowed golden off the recently refinished hardwood floors. "The back half is split into two offices, a bath and a kitchen." Tina moved stiffly down the hallway. "The front half is one large room."

As they stepped into the front area of the building, Reid saw the longing in Tina's eyes as she glanced around the room. A sense of possessiveness, he thought. It suddenly dawned on him why she was upset.

"You wanted this space, didn't you?" he asked quietly. "For yourself."

She stilled at his words, then lifted her chin. "What I wanted is unimportant at this point." She held the key out to him. "The space is yours for one year. Congratulations."

"I'm sorry." He closed his hand around hers as he took the key. Her skin was soft and warm against his. "I didn't know."

"Would it have mattered to you if you had?"

"I wouldn't have changed my mind, if that's what you mean." They both knew he'd be lying if he said anything different. "What were you going to do with it?"

"Nothing that won't keep." Determination shone in her eyes as she glanced around the room. "For another year, anyway. Good luck to you and your father, Mr. Danforth."

When she tried to pull her hand from his, he held tight. Arching one brow, she leveled a questioning gaze at him.

"We are going to be neighbors, Tina," he said. "How 'bout you call me Reid?"

She cocked her head and studied him, and though he wouldn't exactly call it a smile, her mouth wasn't quite so firm, her eyes so cool.

"Good luck, Reid," she said with a nod, then added, "I'll be counting the days."

"So will I, Tina." He grinned at her, then released her hand. "So will I."

From the second-story window of her aunt's apartment, Tina watched the moving van—Miller's Home and Office Rental—pull out of the busy, early-evening traffic and slide into a parking space on the street directly below. A burly, bald-headed man carrying a clipboard and wearing lead-gray overalls stepped out of the van's cab, then disappeared into the first floor.

"Grass certainly doesn't grow under Reid Danforth's feet, does it, Delilah?" Tina said to the long-haired tabby currently winding its sleek, lithe body around her bare legs. "It's hardly been five hours since I handed him a key, and here he is, bringing in furniture.''

Damn him.

Logically, Tina knew she shouldn't blame Reid. It was, after all, her parents' decision. But the fact was, she wasn't feeling especially reasonable—or forgiving—at the moment. Besides, it was much easier to be angry with a stranger than her mother and father.

Tina had made one last-ditch appeal to her mother to reconsider leasing out the space to the Danforths, but her effort had proven futile. Convinced that Abraham Danforth's campaign headquarters would be a hotbed of handsome, wealthy bachelors, Mariska was practically doing handstands.

And speaking of handsome, wealthy bachelors, Tina's pulse jumped when Reid stepped out onto the sidewalk with the burly man.

He'd stripped off the denim jacket he'd been wearing earlier, and looking at his wide shoulders and thick-muscled arms under the T-shirt he wore, she might have thought him one of the movers. When he dropped one large hand on a lean, denim-clad hip and gestured toward the doorway, her eyes traveled downward over his tall, well-sculpted body, then back up again.

She told herself the flutter in her stomach was hunger, not lust.

''Most mothers would warn their daughters about a man like Reid Danforth,'' Tina huffed, then knelt down and picked Delilah up in her arms. ''My mother is already planning a wedding.''

Bored, Delilah twitched her whiskers.

Though she knew she shouldn't be peeping out the blinds, Tina watched Reid walk to the back of the van with the movers. In spite of herself, she couldn't help but admire the confidence that radiated from the man. His stance, his walk, the tilt of his head. Even now, in her mind, she could hear the steady, deep tone of his voice, could feel the firm grasp of his hand over hers.

And that smile, she thought. That smile should be banned from public display.

"All the more reason to stay away from the man," she said emphatically to Delilah. "He knows perfectly well the effect he has on women. I, for one, have no intention of encouraging his already inflated ego."

Still, Tina watched Reid glance at his wristwatch, she could look, couldn't she? As long as he didn't know she was looking, what was the harm?

That's when he glanced up.

With a gasp she jumped back, praying he hadn't been able to see her through the half-open blinds.

Darn it, darn it.

"That's what I get for being nosy," she told Delilah. "And you know what they say about curiosity."

As if annoyed by the comment, Delilah jumped from Tina's arms and strode away with a flick of her pretty tail.

"It's just an expression," Tina called after the cat. "No need to be waspish about it."

Resisting the urge to creep back to the window again, Tina headed for the bathroom, stripped off her work clothes and stepped into the shower. It felt good to let the hot water pound on her shoulders and neck. Slowly, her tension from the day eased.

A year, she told herself. Surely she could manage twelve short months. Fifty-two weeks. She smiled, remembering the look on Reid's face when she'd told him she'd be counting the days. When he'd looked her in the eye and told her he'd be counting them, too, she'd almost felt as if it were a challenge.

God help her, she couldn't resist a challenge.

Yes, you will resist, her mind yelled at her. Determined that she'd spent enough brain space on the man, Tina stuck her head under the spray of water. The time would pass quickly enough. Before she knew it, the man would be out, and she would be in.

The thought lightened her mood immensely.

After she toweled off and passed a blow dryer over her hair, she slipped into a pair of jeans, a pink cotton T-shirt and, because she was going out this evening, a bra. Dinner and a movie with Rachel would take her mind off Reid, Tina told herself.

She found a black leather ankle boot under the end table beside the sofa and was searching for its mate when she heard the sound of muffled voices drifting up from a floor vent. She could almost make out what the men were saying. Was that Reid's voice, too? she wondered, then got down on her hands and knees and listened. They were saying something about turning the desk at an angle.

It was utterly rude to be eavesdropping, of course, and she started to move away until she heard a deep voice say something about the blond babe at the bakery. They were talking about Sophia, Tina knew, but when the man made a crude comment and the rest of the men laughed, Tina gasped.

How dare they talk about her sister like that!

"Hey—" she shouted into the vent "—you down there. That's right, I'm talking to you."

She waited a beat to get their attention, but before she could say anything else, she heard Rachel's voice behind her.

"Tina, what on earth are you doing?"

Startled, she slammed the top of her head on the end table and swore. Rubbing her head, she crawled out backward. "Rachel, for heaven's sake," Tina said, glancing over her shoulder, "you could at least—"

She froze.

Standing next to Rachel, his brow lifted and a smirk on his face, was Reid Danforth.

Please let this be a dream, was her first thought, the next one was to compose herself as quickly as possible.

"—help me look for my shoe," she finished her sentence, though that wasn't what she'd been about to say.

When Reid's gaze drifted down and lingered a moment on her behind, Tina scrambled to her feet.

Why should she be embarrassed he'd caught her on all fours, yelling like a crazy woman down an air vent? He'd invaded her space—again—and she could act any way she wanted. What this man thought about her didn't matter in the slightest.

"Mr. Danforth needs the key to the service panel," Rachel said awkwardly.

"Reid," he corrected Rachel, then smiled.

Rachel blushed and glanced away.

Tina was certain she could bean him with her boot at ten paces and wipe that smile off his face.

"I'm not sure, but I think it's in the kitchen somewhere." Tina hooked an arm through her sister's and smiled. "Rachel, why don't you help me look?"

"I—" Rachel blinked, then met Tina's glare and nodded. "Ah, okay."

When they rounded the corner and were out of sight from Reid, Tina dragged her sister to the laundry room on the opposite side of the kitchen and closed the door. "Why didn't you warn me?"

Rachel furrowed her brow. "Warn you about what?"

"That you were bringing him here," Tina hissed.

"I actually did call, but you didn't answer the phone." Rachel chewed on her bottom lip. "I'm so sorry, T. Did I do something wrong?"

Shame had Tina releasing the tight grip on her sister's arm. "I'm sorry, Rach," she said with a sigh. "I'm just a little upset over losing the space downstairs, that's all. It makes me crazy that Dad and Mom both treat me like a child."

"At least our mother isn't constantly looking to find you a husband, a man that she approves of." Rachel's eyes filled with tears. "Why can't I marry the man I want?"

"You can and you will," Tina said firmly.

"I'm not strong like you," Rachel said quietly. "Or independent like Sophia. I don't know how to say no."

"Then you'll learn." Tina hugged her sister. "We'll go out tonight and work on a—"

Rachel shook her head and stepped away. "I can't go out tonight, T."

"Rachel, if this is because of—"

"I don't want to talk about it." Rachel put up a hand and shook her head. "Please."

"Rachel, please, don't—"

"I've got to go." Rachel wiped away a tear, then opened the door and hurried out of the laundry room.

Frustrated, Tina started to follow, then realized she still had Reid standing in the living room. The key, she remembered. He'd come here for a key to the service box.

She pulled the key from a hook inside the laundry room, drew in a slow breath to steady her nerves, then returned to the living room.

She found him studying the wall where several of her aunt's personal photographs were displayed. Purring loudly, Delilah was weaving her way in and out of Reid's legs. Hussy, Tina thought and frowned at her aunt's cat.

"These pictures are amazing," Reid said when Tina walked into the room. "Your aunt has quite a gift for capturing a mood."

"She's extremely talented." To Delilah's annoyance, Tina scooped the cat up and dropped her on the sofa. "She just had a book of her work published."

"Any of these?"

Tina shook her head. "These are personal. Mostly of my family."

"I like this one of you sitting by the pond reading

a book," he said, pointing to a black-and-white photo. "How old were you?"

It embarrassed her a little, felt strangely intimate looking at photographs of herself with a man she barely knew. Especially Yana's pictures, which seemed to capture the very soul of a person.

"Eighteen, I think." She shrugged. "It was a candid shot, taken with a telephoto lens from my aunt's studio. She's always sneaking around taking pictures of the family when we're not looking. It drives us crazy."

To distract him, she pointed to another picture. "That's my aunt."

"She's a beautiful woman."

With her dark hair and exotic looks, Yana Alexander, even at forty-eight, could still make men forget their own names and stumble over their feet.

"She was in Spain at the time, photographing bull fighters," Tina said. "One of the toreadors took her camera and shot this picture of her."

The man had also been her aunt's lover, Tina knew, but she didn't think she needed to mention that.

"I see a resemblance," Reid said thoughtfully.

It was all she could do not to roll her eyes. She had to give it to him. He was smooth as glass. "I don't look anything like my aunt, Mr. Danforth."

"You have her eyes." He turned to study her face. "And her mouth."

Tina felt her pulse shudder when his gaze lingered on her mouth. *Very smooth.* It irritated her to no end that she was not immune to the man's charm. But, in all fairness to herself, Reid Danforth was certainly not your average man. He was a prime male specimen, with just enough of an edge to make him a touch mysterious.

Working at the bakery, she came into contact with a lot of the local businessmen. Occasionally there'd be an exchange of harmless flirting or innocent banter. She'd even dated a couple of the men. She'd never thought it a big deal or wanted to take it any further.

With Reid, though, something told her it wouldn't be quite so innocent or harmless. Warning flags were waving in her head, signaling her to take another road.

Still, she thought, lifting a brow and meeting his steady gaze, as long as she didn't lose touch with reality—reality being the fact that there was no chance of any kind of relationship between them—then she had no reason to worry. She could hold her own against the likes of Reid Danforth.

She held out the key in her hand. "I believe you came here for this."

"Are you hungry?"

"What?"

"Are you hungry?" he repeated. "I'm going to grab a burger down the street."

Not only smooth, she thought in disbelief, but he moved fast.

But then, she already knew that.

"I made plans." The fact that they'd been changed were none of his business. "But thanks, anyway."

One corner of his mouth tilted up, then he took the key and nodded. "See you tomorrow, T."

She frowned at the closed door after Reid left. How did he know her nickname? Unless…

She glanced at the vent beside the sofa. It *did* back up to the laundry room, she realized. On a groan, she closed her eyes. Had he heard her conversation with Rachel? If he had, then he knew she'd been lying about having plans.

Well, so what if he had? She crossed her arms and pressed her lips together. It wouldn't hurt the man to find out that there might be a few women left in Savannah who weren't completely taken in by that damn smile of his. You're being ridiculous, she told herself. He'd asked her to get a burger with him. That was hardly what anyone would call a date, for heaven's sake.

She knew she was overreacting and decided that was another reason to keep her distance. She'd known him less than a day, and already he'd seriously slanted her equilibrium.

But as she moved past an oval, wood-framed mirror on the wall, she stopped and looked at herself. Her eyes, then her mouth.

Just for a second she wondered.

Oh, for heaven's sake. She shook her head and frowned.

"Idiot," she said out loud, and wasn't certain if she was speaking to herself or Reid.

Three

A cup of coffee in his hand, Reid stepped out of his car the next morning and breathed in the titillating smells wafting on the cool, predawn air. Though the lights were not yet on in the bakery or the Open sign in the window, it was obvious that while most of the city was still sleeping, Ivan Alexander was busy baking for the day ahead.

On the deserted sidewalk, Reid paused and glanced up at Tina's apartment. A soft light edged the closed blinds, and he wondered if she'd already left for work or if she was still up there.

He had an odd feeling that she was.

It was strange, but he'd had the same feeling yesterday, when he'd been standing on the sidewalk with the furniture rental people. The blinds had been partially open, and though he hadn't actually seen her, he'd felt her. Sort of a prickling sensation at the base of his neck.

Weird, he thought, then laughed at himself.

Letting himself in the front door, he flipped on the overhead lights and glanced around. The movers had brought in ten desks yesterday, plus filing cabinets and tables. Phones lines would be hooked up this morning and computers would be installed in the early afternoon. He had set up two private offices in the back, one for himself and one for Nicola. Since she was his father's campaign manager, she'd be the one running the show.

Hands on his hips, he stood in the middle of the room that would soon be filled with volunteers and family and he listened to the absolute quiet.

A floorboard creaked above his head and he looked up, followed the sound across the ceiling. So she *was* upstairs. Leaning back against a desk, he sipped on his coffee and stared at the ceiling.

Had she just gotten out of bed? he wondered. An image of tangled sheets, tousled, golden-brown hair and sleepy eyes came to his mind.

His blood stirred at the thought.

Was she the cotton pajama or silk nightie type? Or maybe, he thought with a smile, she slept in the buff.

That thought stirred more than his blood.

Maybe it was for the best that she'd turned down his offer to get something to eat last night. The woman was a distraction, something he didn't need right now. Something he didn't want.

Still, he thought, listening to the sound of her moving around upstairs, a guy could dream, couldn't he? He took another swig of coffee. No harm in that.

Movement on the sidewalk outside the front window caught Reid's attention. A man who looked familiar hurried past, and Reid recognized him as one of the counter clerks from the bakery. The guy with the blond ponytail. A moment later the sound of a door buzzer filtered down through the vent upstairs. The man hadn't gone to the bakery, Reid realized. He'd gone upstairs.

Reid frowned. A little early to come visiting, wasn't it?

He heard the sound of footsteps moving to the door, muffled voices, then movement again toward—Reid furrowed his brow to remember the layout of the apartment—the sofa, he guessed. Or the bedroom?

Pushing away from the desk, Reid moved closer to the vent and listened. Though it was hard to hear everything, he could distinguish between Tina's voice and the man's, and was able to catch snippets of what they were saying.

"I can't go on like this…" Man's voice.

Tina's voice. "Jason, please be patient and I'm sure we can…"

Man's voice again. "…been patient and nothing has changed…"

Heavy footsteps started, back and forth across the ceiling. The man—Jason—was obviously pacing.

"…a solution," Tina said. "I promise."

Reid concentrated, trying to hear more than bits and pieces of the conversation. He wanted to yell up at them to talk louder.

"I'm going to tell them," Jason said, the frustration heavy in his voice. "We're in love. They'll have to accept it."

Reid went still. Tina and the counter clerk? In love?

The vent was too high to get any closer. He considered dragging a desk chair over and standing on it, but that was a little extreme. Besides, it might be a little difficult to explain if someone saw him with his ear pressed up to the vent.

"...to get to work now," Jason said. "...not giving up."

Footsteps moved back toward the door, then silence.

Confused, Reid stared at the vent for a long moment. He didn't know what, but something wasn't quite on the mark here.

You heard what you heard, pal, a voice in his head said. *Let it go.*

Still...

Oh, hell. He shook his head, wondered why he was having such a difficult time believing that Tina was in love with the bakery clerk. Because of something he'd thought he'd seen in her eyes yesterday? Because of something he'd thought he'd felt when he'd taken her hand in his?

Frowning, he downed the rest of his coffee and crumpled the paper cup in his hand. Maybe it was because he didn't want to believe it. Because he had designs on her himself.

But if she'd been so in love with this guy, then why hadn't she simply said she was seeing someone when he'd asked her out? Reid knew he hadn't exactly been subtle letting her know he was interested.

Who the hell could figure women out? he thought, dragging a hand through his hair. He should be glad she was involved with someone else. He'd known her one day, and already she'd occupied way too much of his brain space. He had a hundred things to do if he was going to have this office up and running by tomorrow. Not one of those things involved a pretty, golden-eyed temptress whose image had kept him awake half the night.

Tossing his crumpled cup into a trash can, he headed for the back office to unload the dozen or so boxes of office supplies that had been delivered yesterday afternoon.

Suddenly, the day—the year—stretching out ahead of him seemed very long, and very boring, indeed.

That entire morning the bell over the bakery door never stopped ringing. Currently a line of customers stretched six deep. Nearly every table and chair were occupied. It wasn't even eleven, Tina realized, and the muffins were gone, the Danish nearly depleted and only a few loaves of bread remained on the shelves.

But still, the biggest seller for the morning at Castle Bakery wasn't baked goods or even the coffee bar, Tina noted while she crammed blue icing into a pastry bag.

It was gossip.

"Mariska Alexander, I declare, y'all must be dizzy with delight." Sharie Jo Sullivan pressed a bag of chocolate *rugala* to her chest, then glanced at her sister, Louzanna. "Imagine, Lulu, right next door to Abraham Danforth's campaign headquarters."

"The *Savannah Morning* calls him Honest Abe II."
Louzanna handed three bills to Mariska, then dug in
her coin purse. "I hear he intends to run a clean, scan-
dal-free campaign."

"What do I know about politics?" Mariska said
with indifference. "They will be good tenants. Anything else is of no interest to me."

Louzanna lifted a dubious brow. "And I suppose
the fact that Abraham's sons and nephews and all
those other eligible bachelors gathered in one place,
no more than a few yards from here, doesn't interest
you, either."

Mariska shrugged, then slowly smiled and leaned
across the counter. "Like fish in a barrel," she said,
wiggling her eyebrows.

The women all laughed.

Tina's grip tightened on the pastry bag, and blue
icing exploded onto the middle of the sheet cake she'd
just frosted. Gritting her teeth, she reached for a knife
to scrape off the errant icing.

"We saw Rachel talking with Reid Danforth on the
sidewalk last night," Sharie Jo whispered. "*After* the
bakery was closed."

Tina glanced over to the coffee bar where Jason was
steaming milk for a latte. Every time Reid's name had
been mentioned this morning—which had been numerous times—Jason's eye had started to twitch. She
wanted to tell him that Reid was no threat to him, but
she knew Jason wouldn't believe her. Especially now,
after listening to the female customers expound on the
Danforth attributes.

Tina could only hope that the novelty would wear

off after a few days and the gossipmongers would find something—or someone—else to occupy their minds. But considering the high profile of the Danforth company, Tina seriously doubted that was going to happen anytime soon. While her mother, Sharie Jo and Louzanna prattled on, Tina forced her attention back to writing "Happy Birthday, Randy" on her cake, determined not to let their conversation bother her.

"All those eligible bachelors," Louzanna said with a sigh. "Ah, if only I was ten years younger."

Sharie Jo rolled her eyes. "Then you'd still be ten years too old."

"Don't be sassy, Sharie Jo," Louzanna said with a sniff, then tucked an imaginary loose strand of blond hair behind her ear. "Besides I wasn't thinking of the younger Danforth men, I was talking about Abraham." Her eyes took on a dreamy quality. "A handsome widow in his fifties. Surely the man must be lonely."

"Don't kid yourself, Lulu," Sharie Jo said. "Rich, powerful, handsome men are never lonely. Bored, maybe. Lonely, no."

In the middle of writing the *t* in birthday, Tina went still. Is that why Reid had asked her out last night? she wondered. Because he was bored? To say that she was different from the women he usually dated was probably the understatement of the century. Blue-blooded Savannah socialites and debutantes were more up his alley. Women with names like Caroline or Blair or—what was the name of the woman in the magazine article she'd plucked from the magazine rack and read this morning? Oh, yeah. She curled one corner of her lip. Mitzi.

Like Sharie Jo said, rich, handsome, powerful men were never lonely. Reid had probably dated dozens of women. Tina shrugged a shoulder, annoyed that she was wasting brain space wondering about the man's love life. Who Reid Danforth did or didn't date certainly had no bearing on her life. They were neighbors for the next year, that was all.

After he'd left her apartment last night, she'd seen him walk across the street and order a pizza at D'mores. Later in the evening, long after she'd gone to bed, she'd heard him working downstairs. She'd done her best to concentrate on the mystery novel she'd been reading, but her mind had kept wandering, wondering what he was doing.

Wondering what might have happened if she had gone out with him.

"Maybe I would have been the one bored," she muttered out loud.

"Did you say something, Katina?" Mariska glanced over.

"No," she said quickly. "Nothing at all."

When her mother turned back to her customers, Tina shook her head at her foolishness. She doubted Reid even remembered her name today, and here she was, talking to herself about the man.

Determined not to let thoughts of Reid Danforth distract her further, she finished the *y* in Randy, then looked at her work.

Happy Birtday, Randy.

Birtday?

So much for her determination not to be distracted.

Scowling, she reached for the knife again to fix her mistake, then added more white frosting to smooth the top of the cake. Completely focused now, she grabbed the pastry bag and concentrated on her work.

When every letter was perfect, Tina gave a satisfied nod. Lifting the pastry bag to dot the *i,* she happened to glance over as Reid walked in the door.

His gaze met hers and held, and though it was only for a moment, it felt like minutes. Hours. If a fire had broken out and she was surrounded by flames, she couldn't have moved.

When one corner of his mouth lifted, her heart did a somersault, her hand tightened.

And blue icing oozed all over her cake.

Chastising herself, she looked away. Darn it! She'd been so proud of herself that she'd managed to resist the man's charm, then he walks in the door with that you-want-me-you-know-you-do grin, and suddenly she can't breathe? How did he do that? she thought irritably.

Every head had turned. Conversation had died. When he walked through the crowd, it was like someone had rolled out a red carpet. And when he flashed that smile on the women in the bakery, they all but swooned.

He owned the room, Tina realized. His confidence, his demeanor, his presence. And his looks, she thought, appreciating the stretch of broad shoulders under his black polo shirt and the low slung worn jeans across lean hips and long legs. A woman didn't stand a chance.

Well, except her, of course.

It took all of five seconds for the bakery to erupt into chaos and converge on Reid, another forty-five seconds for Tina's mother to come around the counter and push her way through the crowd like a linebacker at the Super Bowl.

"Let the man sit." Mariska shooed everyone away. "Jason, bring our new neighbor a cup of coffee."

When Jason mumbled something under his breath, Tina shot him a warning glance. Nothing but trouble and heartache would come from any kind of public confrontation between the two men. A scowl on his face, Jason turned away, certainly not appeased, but for the moment, at least, contained.

"Thank you." Reid plucked a ticket from the number machine. "But I can wait my turn."

"Of course you will not wait," Mariska said and everyone who still had tickets in their hand nodded their approval. "Latte, cappuccino, espresso?"

Tina rolled her eyes, surprised her mother didn't add, *my daughter's hand in marriage?*

"Black would be great," Reid said. "But—"

"We have strudel still warm from the oven." Mariska didn't give Reid a chance to protest as she pulled him to a chair. "Tina, a slice of strudel for Mr. Danforth. And a nice apricot *rugala.*"

"Please, call me Reid," he said to Mariska, then looked at Tina with a grin that clearly said he was enjoying himself. "I really don't want to be any trouble."

"It is no trouble," Mariska said cheerfully. "Is it, Katina?"

Though it hurt, Tina smiled. "No, of course not. No trouble at all."

"So tell me." Mariska sat in the chair beside Reid. "Will your wife be helping you with the campaign?"

Oh, for heaven's sake. Tina turned to slice the strudel. Her mother couldn't have been less subtle if she'd pulled out a calendar and asked him what day he was available to plan a small wedding for four or five hundred.

"I don't have a wife," Reid said. "But I'm certainly looking for volunteers."

Tina's head shot up. Every female in the room drew in a breath.

But before Mariska—or any of the other women in the room—could offer their services, Reid said, "To help with the campaign, of course."

Disappointment rippled through the bakery.

"Ah." Mariska's shoulders sagged, then straightened again as she smiled brightly. "My daughters will help," she said with enthusiasm. "We are all big supporters, you know."

What! Since when were they supporters of any political campaign? Tina stared at her mother in horror.

"That's very generous of you, Mrs. Alexander." Reid slid a glance at Tina. "But maybe you should ask your daughters how they feel about that."

"Sophia and Rachel will be happy to volunteer," Mariska said, waving a don't-be-silly hand at him. Then she added as an afterthought, "And my Tina, of course."

Tina clenched her jaw at the murmurs and nods from the customers who weren't even pretending not to listen. It wasn't bad enough she'd lost out on her restaurant to Reid and his family, now she was supposed to *help* them? She had to stop her mother before this got out of hand. Snatching up the plate of strudel and the cup of coffee Jason had poured, Tina hurried over to the table.

"Mom," she said as sweetly as she could muster. "I'm sure Mr. Danforth is looking for volunteers with some political knowledge."

"Not at all." Leaning back in his chair, Reid glanced up at her. "We're having a volunteer welcome gathering tomorrow night at seven-thirty. Why don't you and your sisters come by?"

Tina opened her mouth to say she was busy, but her mother was much too fast.

"They will be there. We will all be there," Mariska said firmly. "I will bring cookies and *rugala.*"

When Mariska rose, Reid stood, as well, smiling as he extended his hand. "Thank you, Mrs. Alexander. You are an extremely generous woman."

When Reid smiled, Mariska's cheeks bloomed red and she giggled. Tina's jaw went slack. Her mother never blushed, and she most certainly did not giggle. Disgusted, Tina watched her mother hurry back into the kitchen.

Did all the Danforth men have the ability to make women act and feel stupid? she wondered, glancing back at Reid. If they did, Tina could only hope that one day some brilliant female scientist would be able to isolate that gene and come up with a vaccination.

She'd be first in line.

"Your strudel," she said tightly, sliding the plate onto the table and setting the coffee beside it.

"Thanks."

"Don't mention it."

When she turned, he surprised her by reaching for her arm. *Darn it.* There it was again. That jolt of electricity. She looked at him, prayed he couldn't feel it, too. Prayed that he couldn't see the effect he had on her. With so many people watching, it would really be embarrassing if she swooned.

"Here." He took her hand and laid a key in her palm. "I had a copy made."

To anyone watching it was a completely innocent exchange. To Tina it felt personal. The touch of his fingertips on her skin, the press of the key in her palm. The almost imperceptible lingering of his hand against her own.

She closed her fingers tightly around the key and pulled her hand away. "Thanks."

"Till tomorrow, then," he said with a nod.

"Right. Tomorrow." When she turned and walked away, she could have sworn she heard him chuckle.

She hoped he choked on the strudel.

Lying on his back under the desk, Reid struggled to wiggle the printer cable into the back of the computer. If he'd had another inch of cable, along with another inch of space to reach into, he would have been done ten minutes ago.

But that would have been easy, he thought irritably. And after the morning he'd had, why should he expect his afternoon to be any better?

He'd scraped his knuckles changing a flat tire, dropped a cup of coffee on the press release he'd told Nicola he'd fax to the *Savannah Morning News,* misplaced the sign-in book for the orientation tonight and just five minutes ago, reaching blindly into the back of the desk, drove a splinter the size of a screwdriver under his thumbnail.

It still hurt like hell, dammit.

But what really aggravated him the most, what really set his teeth on edge, was the slender, curvy, sassy-mouthed woman he couldn't get out of his mind.

What was it about Tina Alexander that had him tied up in knots? he wondered. With her velvet, amber-brown eyes, heart-shaped face and turned-up nose she was pretty, but not necessarily what most men would consider beautiful. She was average height, a little thin for his taste and icy as an Arctic breeze.

Damn if he didn't want to get his hands on her.

It was as if she'd gone out of her way to alienate him, and perhaps that was what intrigued him the most. But he wasn't stupid, and he certainly wasn't blind. He'd seen the way she'd reacted every time he'd touched her. He'd felt her shiver, watched her eyes widen. Something told him that under that cool exterior was heat and plenty of it.

Damn if he didn't want to taste that heat.

When the cable slipped from his fingers for the tenth time in fifteen minutes, he swore like a truck driver in a skid, then narrowed his eyes and threaded the cable through the hole in the wall of the desk again. He'd be damned if he'd let a stubborn printer cable—or woman—make him lose control.

When the cable plug finally dropped over the inlet, Reid smiled, grabbed his bottom lip between his teeth while he wiggled the cable into place...

"Hello?"

At the sound of the feminine greeting, Reid sat up sharply and slammed the top of his head on the underside of the desk. He wasn't certain if the crack he heard was wood or his skull.

Dammit, dammit, dammit...

Through the stars swimming in his blurred vision, Reid watched a pair of shapely legs appear from around the corner of the desk.

"Sorry if I startled you." Tina peered down at him. "You okay?"

Grunting, he pulled himself from under the desk, winced at the rocket of pain that shot through his brain when he sat. "Sure. I slam my head into desks every day just for fun."

His sarcasm earned him a smile. She dropped down on her knees and leaned close. "Here, let me look."

"I'm fine." When she reached out and took his head in her hands, his heart slammed against his ribs.

"I don't see any blood," she said, gently sliding her fingers through his hair.

That's because it's all dropped to the lower half of my body, Reid wanted to say, but wasn't willing to risk her letting go of him just yet.

His head tingled; heat rushed through his veins. He'd never felt anything like it before. Maybe I'm hallucinating, he thought. Or maybe he'd knocked himself out and this was one hell of an erotic dream.

If so, he didn't want to wake up.

"Where does it hurt?" she asked.

Her fingernails lightly brushed over his scalp, and Reid's throat turned to dust. He doubted he'd be able to speak if he tried, so he simply pointed.

"I did knock," she said, softly touching the area he'd indicated. "I guess you didn't hear me."

He could barely hear her now, through the buzzing in his head.

"The door was open," she went on when he didn't respond. "I thought maybe you were in the back."

When her fingertips moved in a soothing, circular motion, Reid bit back a groan. Less than a foot separated their bodies; the press of her breasts against the white blouse she wore made it difficult to breathe, let alone think.

Surely the torture this woman was putting him through had to be some kind of karmic payback for something he'd done in his life, Reid thought. Some wrong he'd caused someone. The sweet scent of her—a mix of vanilla and cinnamon—the soft, incredibly erotic touch of her hands, the seductive, provocative tone of her voice. It was all he could do not to drag her in his arms, right here under this desk, on this dusty floor, to taste her, to shove her skirt up those long, slender legs until he touched warm, soft flesh and—

Gritting his teeth, he clamped his hands around her wrists. He didn't pull her to him. He didn't push her away.

Her eyes widened; her lips parted with surprise. She didn't move.

He held her gaze with his own. Slowly, his intent clear, he tugged her closer...closer....

When his mouth touched hers, he watched her lashes flutter down, felt the release of her breath on his cheek. Her lips were soft as rose petals. He nibbled, cautiously, lightly, eager to taste her more fully. And while she didn't respond, she didn't pull away, either.

It was all the encouragement he needed.

He deepened the kiss, though just barely, tracing her bottom lip with his tongue. Sweet, he thought. Unbelievably, seductively sweet.

He wasn't at all surprised at the need coursing through his body; he'd been attracted to her from the beginning, had wanted this since he'd laid eyes on her. Nor was he surprised by her response. He'd sensed her attraction to him, as well.

What surprised—no, annoyed—him was the unexpected, niggling question chipping away at the edge of his desire.

"What would Jason think about this?" he murmured the words, cursed himself for wanting to know.

She stilled, then her eyes slowly opened. "Jason?"

"Yeah," he said dryly. "Remember him?"

Confusion furrowed her brow, then suspicion. "What do you know about Jason?"

"Not much." Obviously, she didn't appreciate being reminded that she and Jason were an item while she was kissing another man, Reid thought irritably. "I was hoping you would tell me."

It was fascinating, as well as frustrating, to watch the heat in Tina's eyes turn to ice. With a regal lift of her chin, she pulled back, then stood and smoothed the front of her skirt. "I was sent over here to find out how many people to expect this evening."

"Look, I'm sorry." Reid stood, reached for her arm, but she yanked it away. "I shouldn't have—"

"Fifty?" she said coolly. "A hundred?"

"Around fifty." He dragged a hand through his hair, was instantly reminded of the bump he'd taken. "Tina, dammit, I know it's none of my business, I—"

"You got that right, mister," she said, tossing her hair back over her shoulders. "Now if you'll excuse me, I really need to get back to work."

Reid watched her turn on her heel and march stiffly out the door.

"Smooth, Danforth," he muttered. "Real smooth."

Resting a hip on the desk, Reid stared at the door Tina had just disappeared through. It would be easier to just let it go, he told himself, to forget about her and keep his mind completely focused on his work.

But, he thought, smiling slowly, remembering the feel of her mouth against his, it wouldn't be nearly as interesting.

Four

Tina didn't make it to the alley before her knees buckled. Struggling to breathe, she stumbled around the corner of the passageway between the buildings and leaned against the wall.

Reid had kissed her.

She'd kissed him back.

Closing her eyes, she laid her head against the cool bricks. A groan rolled deep in her throat.

And what a kiss.

Her lips still tingled, her head still reeled, her pulse raced. She glanced down at the tips of her shoes to see if smoke was rising.

She'd certainly been kissed before, she wasn't completely inexperienced with men. But she'd never been kissed like that. Never been so overwhelmed. And if he hadn't asked her that ridiculous question about Jason, she'd probably be rolling around on the floor with Reid at this very moment.

The thought made her cheeks burn.

She wasn't certain if she was glad that they'd stopped before things heated up even more, or if she was irritated.

Of course I'm glad, she thought, narrowing her eyes. Deliriously glad.

She touched her mouth. She could still taste him there, could still feel the press of his mouth on hers. An involuntary shudder coursed through her, and she knew she'd be lying if she didn't at least admit she'd been curious. And maybe, at an unconscious level, she'd actually *wanted* him to kiss her. After all, she *had* been the one who'd touched him first. He must have thought she'd been asking—begging—for it, the way she'd put her hands on his head, then combed her fingers through his hair and lightly stroked his head.

Remembering the soft, thick texture of his hair sliding through her fingers and the touch of his scalp under her fingernails sent a wave of heat shimmering over her skin. She still couldn't believe she'd done something so...*intimate*.

Couldn't believe her fingers itched to do it again.

A welcome breeze rippled through the alley, cooling her blood and her skin, finally bringing her overloaded senses back to a manageable level. Once again, reason prevailed.

You're making too big a deal about this, she told herself. Men like Reid kissed women all the time. It didn't mean anything to him, for heaven's sake, and it shouldn't mean anything to her, either.

"It doesn't," she said, needing to hear herself say it out loud. Reid had caught her off guard, that was all. In the future, she'd be more careful around him.

She'd also have to warn Jason to be more careful, she realized. If her parents found out about him—Tina shuddered at the thought—there would be hell to pay.

But there was no reason for them to find out, she told herself. Reid didn't know anything. He'd been fishing, and he'd come up with an empty hook.

She intended to keep it that way.

At seven forty-five that evening, Abraham Danforth's campaign headquarters had officially been open for fifteen minutes. The scent of fresh-brewed coffee and still-warm cookies wafted through the already crowded room. Music, upbeat instrumentals meant more to inspire than entertain, flowed from an overhead sound system, but could barely be heard over the excited conversations of volunteers and newly hired campaign staff. Because the man of the hour hadn't arrived yet, anticipation increased with each passing minute.

Reid, arms folded, leaning against the back wall of the room, watched the activity buzzing around him. His family was scattered throughout the room: Kimberly sat at a guest book table; Adam manned the volunteer schedule; his cousin Jake was currently charming Matilda Henning, the president of the Savannah Women's Historical League. Nicola Granville, wearing an Honest Abe II campaign button on the lapel of her navy blue blazer and a straw Danforth for Senator hat tucked neatly over her red hair, made her way through the throng of people and personally greeted each and every one of them.

Abraham might be the heart of the campaign, but the volunteers were the lifeblood. Without them, no amount of publicity or money could win an election.

But there was really only one volunteer—albeit a reluctant one—that had caught Reid's attention and he shifted his gaze to Tina.

Wearing tan linen slacks and a black turtleneck, she stood by the refreshment table with Jason, a cup of punch in her hand, listening politely to an animated, balding man dressed in an oversize gray suit. She appeared cool and composed and even interested in what the man was saying to her, but when he turned away from her to grab another cookie from a tray, Tina's boredom flashed in her eyes.

Reid smiled, even considered saving her. It would be easy to make his way over there and tell her she had a phone call in the back office. But he wasn't so sure she would appreciate the gesture, not with Jason standing there, and especially not after what had happened between them this afternoon.

Not that he was really sure what had happened. He'd kissed her, she'd kissed him back, they'd both enjoyed it—that much he knew. Everything else was just a little fuzzy. Maybe he had hit his head too hard, he thought, though it certainly hadn't knocked any sense into him.

Because all he'd thought about since he'd kissed her was kissing her again.

From the moment Tina had walked into campaign headquarters with Rachel and Jason a few minutes ago, Reid had been very aware of the fact that she'd kept her distance from him. She hadn't even glanced in his direction. It would certainly make sense that with her boyfriend here, she might want to avoid the man she'd been in a lip lock with just a few hours earlier.

But what she couldn't avoid was the unspoken tension still lingering between them. It didn't matter that she was on the other side of the room, it was there nonetheless. He knew it, and he knew that she knew it, too.

Whether she would admit it or not was another issue.

"A friend of yours?"

Reid turned at the sound of Ian's voice, annoyed that his brother had caught him staring. "Who?"

Ian took a sip of his coffee, then grinned that annoying I'm-your-brother-you-can't-fool-me grin. "Not the type you usually go for, is she?"

Refusing to answer his question or rise to the bait, Reid simply lifted a brow. "And exactly what type is it you seem to think I go for?"

"Dim-witted debutantes," Ian said, cocking his head. "High-society heiresses, soporific society girls."

Reid frowned. So maybe a few of the women he'd dated had been a little shallow, he thought irritably. Or maybe just a little low in the brain cell department. So what? He'd been looking for company, not commitment. And Ian, of all people, who'd avoided any kind of relationship since his divorce, was hardly one to talk.

"For your information," Reid said dryly, "her father owns Castle Bakery."

"Ah. One of the Alexander daughters." Ian nodded, then sipped his coffee again as he glanced across the room at Tina. "Jake and I have talked about adding some new items to D&D's. Maybe I should go introduce myself."

Reid slid a dark look at his brother. "She's not on the menu, Ian."

"Is that so?" Grinning, Ian returned his attention to Reid. "Not on my menu or yours?"

Reid would have liked nothing better than to wipe that smirk off his brother's face, but considering the time and place, it would have to wait. "Neither. She has a boyfriend."

Ian shrugged. "I don't see any ring on her finger. You getting soft in your old age?"

"Why don't we go out back and see who's soft?" Reid said irritably.

"You're too pretty in that new suit to mess up." Ian slapped a good-natured hand on Reid's shoulder. "And besides, I hear she's got sisters. Good Lord, please tell me that's one of them."

Reid followed the direction of his brother's gaze. The tall, leggy blonde had just stepped through the front door. Curls spilled from a silver clip on top of her head and tumbled around an oval face, lush mouth and pale-green eyes. The long-sleeved ruffled blouse and black leather pants she wore showed off a body that most men could only fantasize about.

And right now, Reid noted, just about every man in the room was doing some serious fantasizing.

"Daughter number one, Sophia," Reid said. He'd met her yesterday at the bakery. "Why don't you go introduce yourself?"

Keeping his eyes on the blonde, Ian straightened his tie, then handed Reid his coffee. "I think I'll do that."

Reid watched his brother move in on Sophia like a panther, but he had the feeling that the woman could handle herself. He took a moment to appreciate her beauty—he was human, after all—but it simply wasn't the eldest Alexander daughter he was preoccupied with at the moment.

And even though he didn't want to admit it, not even to himself, he knew that Ian had been right about Tina. She *was* different from the other women he'd dated or been interested in before. It was strange how she annoyed and fascinated him at the same time. Something about her had caught his attention and refused to let go. Despite his better judgment, he intended to explore what that something was.

"May I have everyone's attention, please," Nicola said over the noise in the room, then waited until the crowd slowly quieted. "I'd like to thank you all for coming this evening. I speak for Abraham and myself when I say how grateful we are to each and every one of you for so generously donating your time and money to this campaign. With your support, there is no doubt in our minds and hearts who the next senator of our beautiful state of Georgia will be—Abraham Danforth!"

Cheers and applause exploded from the crowd, and a few zealous volunteers held up Honest Abe II bumper stickers that Nicola had distributed a few minutes ago.

"And a special thank you," Nicola said when the crowd quieted down, "to Ivan and Mariska Alexander from Castle Bakery for so generously providing refreshments for us this evening."

Mariska beamed and waved at everyone, while Ivan, clearly not liking the attention, nodded stiffly.

"At this time I'd like to invite everyone to mark the date for a cocktail party at Crofthaven in two weeks." Nicola waited for the excited murmur to settle down, then smiled and went on, "For now, while we're waiting for Abraham to arrive, please help yourself to drinks and desserts and introduce yourself to your fellow volunteers."

Reid sipped on the coffee his brother had left him while the crowd moved in on the sweets. And speaking of sweet...Reid glanced back to where he'd seen Tina standing a few minutes ago, but she was gone. Slowly he scanned the crowd, but didn't see her amongst the mass of people crowded in the room.

He didn't see Jason, either.

They hadn't gone out the front door, Reid was certain of that. Which meant they'd either gone into the back offices, rest room or out the back door.

What the hell does it matter? he thought, though he already knew the answer. It did matter, dammit. And he was suddenly in a bad mood because he didn't want it to.

If she and Jason really were an item, then fine. But if that were true, Reid asked himself, then why, just a few hours ago, had she been kissing *me?* And why, when he'd asked her point-blank what the deal was, had she turned so indignant?

Something didn't jibe. Reid wasn't certain what it was, but once and for all, he wanted an answer.

It took several minutes to make his way through the crowd, but when he finally stepped into the back hallway, Reid could see the offices and the rest room were empty.

Questioning his sanity, not to mention his lack of common sense, he stepped outside.

The air was crisp, the cloudless night sky filled with stars. An iridescent ring shimmered around a nearly full moon. In the far distance, a ship's horn sounded from the river. A perfect night for a tryst, Reid thought, closing the door behind him.

When he saw the couple standing in the shadows of the garden, their arms entwined, Reid's hands balled into fists and he nearly turned back around. But then he heard Ian's voice in his head, accusing him of being soft. Like hell I am.

Relaxing his hands, he shoved them into his pockets and strolled casually over. "Nice evening."

The couple jumped apart. Jason stepped in front of the woman in his arms, shielding her from view. "We were just...getting a little fresh air."

Why the hell was Tina hiding behind this guy? Reid wondered. The woman he'd met wasn't the type to cower in a corner when confronted. Unless she was worried about Jason finding out she'd been kissing another man.

"Sorry if I interrupted." In an attempt to see around

Jason, Reid moved a couple feet to the left. Jason moved, too.

"No problem," Jason said, though his voice gave away his nervousness.

"Look." Reid sighed. "Why don't we just—"

"What in the world are you doing out here? Are you crazy?"

Startled at the sound of Tina's hushed shout from behind him, Reid turned. She hurried across the patio toward them. Confused, Reid looked back at Jason, then watched a woman step hesitantly from the shadows.

Rachel.

"Mom is looking for you both," Tina said to her sister. "You've got to get back inside before—"

"What is going on out here?"

At the sound of her mother's voice, Tina froze, then slowly turned. Hands on her hips, eyes narrowed suspiciously, Mariska looked at the group assembled on the patio.

"I was just—" Tina faltered. "We were just—"

"Rachel said she had a headache," Reid said easily as he moved closer to Rachel. "I brought her out here for some fresh air."

Stunned, Tina looked at Reid, wasn't quite sure why he was lying for them, but was thankful nonetheless.

"That's right," Tina added quickly. "Jason and I just came out to see how she's doing."

"Oh." Mariska glanced from Rachel to Reid, then her eyes widened with delight. "*Ohh.* I see. Yes, well, fresh air is good for a headache, is it not?"

Nodding, Rachel glanced hesitantly at Reid, then smiled stiffly. "I...I'm feeling much better now."

Her mother was obviously hearing wedding bells, Tina knew. What her mother didn't know, was that she was looking at the wrong groom.

"Well, then," Mariska said, already turning. "I will just go back inside and tell your father that you are all right."

"We'll be right there," Reid called after her.

When Mariska disappeared back inside, Jason glared at Reid, then took Rachel's hand in a blatant display of possessiveness. "Rachel, we've got to settle this now. I'll talk to your parents and—"

"No." Rachel pulled her hand from Jason's, then looked at Reid. "We didn't mean to involve you. I'm sorry."

Tears shining in her eyes, Rachel quickly followed after her mother. Jason started after her.

"Jason." Tina touched his shoulder and shook her head. "Please. Not now."

Jason stopped; a muscle jumped in his jaw. Shaking off Tina's hand, he turned on his heel and stomped out the side garden gate, slamming it behind him.

Tina slowly released the breath she'd been holding. That had been close. Too close. Forcing a smile, she turned to Reid. "Thank you. You have no idea what kind of disaster you just diverted."

"Why don't you tell me?"

Though her first impulse was to hold back, Tina reminded herself he had helped, after all. She supposed she at least owed him the truth. "Jason and Rachel are in love."

The look he gave her said, "Duh."

"Rachel doesn't like confrontation," Tina explained. "She knows my parents wouldn't approve of her dating Jason, so they've kept it a secret."

"Why wouldn't they approve?"

"For one thing, he's an employee. That's always been absolutely forbidden."

"So why doesn't he just quit?"

"It's not that simple." Tina sighed. "He's also the lead singer in a band called Controversy."

"The struggling musician," Reid said thoughtfully.

"A double whammy," Tina said with a nod. "Even if he quit the bakery, my parents still wouldn't approve. And Rachel won't let him quit the band. She knows how much his music means to him."

"Is he any good?"

"Rachel says so." Tina hugged herself when a cold breeze swirled leaves around her feet. "But it's a tough business."

"You're cold." Reid shrugged out of his suit jacket and dropped it over her shoulders. "Here."

"No, really, I'm fine, you don't have to—"

When he took hold of the lapels and tugged her closer, Tina's protest died on her lips. She could feel his warmth inside the jacket, could smell his masculine scent on the brushed wool. When he tugged her closer still, her pulse skipped, then raced.

"When I came out here tonight," he said, gazing down at her, "I thought you were the woman Jason was kissing."

If she'd had any air left in her lungs, Tina might have laughed. "Me?"

He nodded. "I thought you two were involved."

She did laugh now, though it was such a throaty, deep sound that she wondered where it came from. "That's why you asked me about Jason earlier, after—" She stopped, felt her cheeks heat up.

"After you kissed me," he murmured.

"I kissed *you?*" Lifting an indignant brow, she angled her head and met his dark gaze. "That's not the way I remember it."

"Yeah?" His gaze dropped to her mouth. "How do you remember it?"

Ignoring the voice in her head that told her to run, Tina placed her palms flat on Reid's chest and leaned into him. She felt the steady thud of his heart under her fingertips and the heat of his skin through his cotton dress shirt. "Remember what?"

Smiling, he lowered his mouth to hers.

It was the same as before. The same wild rush. The same build of heat.

The same insanity.

His lips moved over hers, gently at first, barely tasting. Certainly not a kiss that should overwhelm or overpower, she thought dimly. Nothing that should make her knees weak or her mind numb.

But it did all of those things. All that and more.

A lot more.

He changed the angle of the kiss, traced the seam of her lips with his tongue, then dipped inside to meet hers. Her breath caught, quickened. He tasted like coffee, dark and rich and hot. His hands slid inside his jacket and around her waist, pulling her body flush with his. His thumbs brushed over her rib cage, no more than a whisper from the underside of her breasts. Desire shot through her like an arrow, hummed deep in her throat.

Afraid she might sink to the ground if she didn't hold tight, Tina slid her hands upward. His shoulders were wide and strong; she felt the ripple of muscle as she circled his neck with her arms.

A tiny part of her brain fought to regain control of reason. This could go nowhere, could lead to nothing but heartache, that tiny voice screamed at her. She'd be way in over her head with a man like Reid. But it seemed that her body had a mind of its own, determined to enjoy the moment, consequences be damned.

When he deepened the kiss, when the tips of his thumbs barely brushed the curve of her breasts, even that tiny voice shut up. She heard the sound of her own soft moan, but was too immersed in the sensations swirling through her to be embarrassed. His touch thrilled her, consumed her, and she knew she was lost.

Reid felt the shudder roll through her body into his. He was no stranger to desire, to need, but this was something different, something stronger, deeper, than anything he'd experienced before. The urgency grew like a storm, dark and swirling, heavy. His pulse pounded in his head, in his body.

Lifting his head, he gazed down at her, watched her slowly open her eyes. Passion smoldered there. Her lips, swollen and moist, enticed him to dip down and taste her again.

"So sweet," he murmured against her lips. "So soft."

Desperately he wanted to drag Tina upstairs to her aunt's apartment and finish what they'd started here, but the faint sound of laughter from inside the building reminded him where they were. Frustration had him tightening his hold on her, then mentally cursing his lack of timing.

With a willpower he didn't know he possessed, he pulled away, then pressed his forehead to hers.

"We should go back inside," he said with a sigh.

She blinked. "What?"

"My father will be arriving any minute," he explained. "They'll wonder where I am."

"Oh, yes, of course." She stepped back, slipped his jacket from her shoulders and handed it to him. "Thanks."

"Tina—"

"It's no big deal, Reid." She tilted her head and smiled. "We got a little caught up in the moment, that's all. It happens."

It happens? Annoyance tapped at his pride. "Twice now, if you're counting," he said dryly, and she at least gave him the satisfaction of appearing embarrassed.

"I...I'm sorry." She dropped her gaze and folded her arms. "I'm not handling this well at all. I just don't want to give you the wrong impression, that's all."

"And what impression was that?"

"That I—that we—" She shifted awkwardly. "That this would go anywhere."

"So what you're trying to say is," he said, keeping his voice even, holding her gaze and watching her eyes widen as he stepped close to her, "you aren't going to sleep with me."

She drew in a slow breath. "No."

"No, you aren't trying to say that?"

"No—I mean, yes." Flustered, she shook her head. "I'm not going to sleep with you."

"The thing is, Tina." He touched her earlobe with his fingertip, heard her soft intake of breath. "I haven't asked."

Thoroughly satisfied at the surprise in her eyes, Reid dropped his hand.

"See you inside," he said casually, then wished to God he could see the look on her face as he strolled away.

Five

———

Saturday afternoon, with her shift finished and the bakery closed, Tina made her way up the stairs to her aunt's apartment. All day she'd been dreaming of a quiet evening at home. Alone. In her mind she'd planned an hour-long bubble bath, with scented candles and a glass of white wine. Next came her favorite sweatpants, a cotton tank top, soft slippers and the mystery novel she'd started two weeks ago.

And maybe, just maybe, she might even get some sleep, instead of tossing and turning all night thinking about Reid.

Her cheeks still burned every time she remembered what he'd said to her last night before he'd walked away. *I haven't asked.*

She'd managed to get through the rest of the evening, had even smiled and held her voice steady when her mother had dragged her over to meet Abraham Danforth. It was like looking at an older version of Reid. The same piercing deep-blue eyes, the same thick, sable-brown hair. The same charm. Like Reid, he exuded power and masculinity. And like Reid, the women, young and old, couldn't take their eyes off him. Suddenly Tina completely understood why Reid hadn't asked her to sleep with him.

Because he didn't have to.

He had his pick of any woman he wanted. Anytime.

Tina knew she was no femme fatale. Men might have shown an interest in her from time to time, but they weren't exactly dropping at her feet.

So the question she'd asked herself repeatedly since she'd met Reid was, why is he interested in me?

Still mulling that thought over, she slipped her key into the lock and opened the door.

In front of her eyes, Tina's dreams of a quiet evening dissolved like sugar in water.

"Tina, it's so wonderful." Rachel met her at the door and dragged her inside the apartment. "You won't believe what Sophie's done."

Rachel glanced at Sophia, who was sitting on the sofa, making an old pair of jeans and oversize white tunic top look like high fashion. She had an incredibly smug look on her face. "Swallowed the canary?"

"No, silly." Excitement danced in Rachel's eyes. "She got Jason's band booked at Steam. Tonight!"

Tina stared wide-eyed at Rachel, then Sophia. Steam was the newest, hottest, most-difficult-to-get-into blues dinner and night club in Savannah. Though Tina had never been there herself, she knew that Sophia went often, that she'd even done some interior designing in the owner's office.

Tina also knew that it took nothing short of a miracle for a band to get a booking there. "And how, pray tell, did you manage that one?"

Sophia casually shrugged a shoulder, but there was a twinkle of a smile in her eyes. "The band booked for tonight had to cancel. The owner owes me a favor."

Tina lifted a curious brow. "What kind of favor?"

"Not that kind, dear," Sophia said with a pretty tilt of her head. "Though Clay Crawford is quite a catch. We just decided we'd make better friends."

"Could we please not discuss Sophia's love life for once." Rachel took hold of Tina's hand and pulled her to the sofa. "We have to talk about what we're going to wear."

"We?" Tina swiveled a look at Rachel.

"Of course 'we,'" Rachel said. "I told Jason we'd all be there. And this is the perfect night for us all to go out with no questions from Mom and Dad."

Saturday night was her parents' date night out to Buddy's Buffet and Bingo on the waterfront. Unless one of them was sick, they never missed it. It was the perfect night for her and her sisters to all go out and not have to worry about any inquisitions. Tina's fantasy of a bubble bath began to pop, one scented bubble after the other.

"Just think." Rachel clasped her hands to her chest. "Jason, my Jason, singing at Steam! You have to come, Tina."

The happiness on her sister's face disintegrated the

last of Tina's resolve. "Of course I'm coming," she said, surprised at her own sudden rush of excitement. "I wouldn't miss it."

"I love you both so much!" Laughing, Rachel threw her arms around Tina and Sophia. "This will be the best night of my life!"

Maybe this was exactly what she needed, Tina reasoned. She hadn't been out with her sisters like this in a long time. A little music, a little wine. It would be fun. Maybe she'd meet someone nice. Someone who could make her forget about Reid Danforth.

Who knows, she thought, maybe this would be her lucky night.

Starting at nine every night of the week, Steam featured only the best in live blues music. On a Saturday night, without a reservation or a connection, it was nearly impossible to get in either the posh second-floor restaurant or the trendy club on the first floor.

Unless, of course, your last name was Danforth.

"Are you dining this evening, Mr. Danforth?" The hostess, a pretty brunette in a black cocktail dress smiled at Reid. "Or would you like a table in the club?"

"In the club." Smiling back at the woman, Reid slipped her a bill that made her eyes widen. With the skill of a magician, the money disappeared. "I'm meeting my brother."

"Thank you, sir. Just give me one moment to find the best seat for you."

While the hostess scribbled on a seating chart in front of her, Reid took in the decor of the large, dimly lit reception area. Deep-red velvet draperies hung from the floor-to-ceiling windows; the walls were pale gray, with thin red stripes. A lavish Oriental rug in hues of red, gray and black graced the highly polished, dark mahogany floor. Behind the hostess, a large mahogany staircase led to the restaurant upstairs. To the right, the bar area vibrated with conversation and laughter.

"Right this way, sir."

Still not certain why Ian had insisted on meeting him here tonight, Reid followed the hostess through an entrance to the left which led to the stage and dance area. "Let's Give Them Something to Talk About" blasted from the dj's speakers and bodies moved on the dance floor in rhythm to Bonnie Raitt's raspy tune while cocktail waitresses in black slacks and button-down red blouses hustled through the crowd, balancing trays and taking orders.

Settling in at a stage side table, Reid ordered a beer then munched on a spicy mix of pretzels and nuts the waitress had left him. Since his college days, he'd spent very little time in night clubs and bars, but some things never changed. And though Steam was much too high class for the average college frat boys, the draw was still the same: music, food, drink and, of course, the women.

He glanced around the packed room at the slinky dresses and low-cut tops. A great deal of skin and cleavage were on display, and he'd have to be dead not to notice it. Still, other than a mild flicker of appreciation, he wasn't interested in engaging any of the glances a few of the women were sliding his way.

It irritated the hell out of him that he couldn't get

Tina out of his mind. Frustrated him to no end that since he'd kissed her, all he could think about was kissing her again.

And more.

At least he knew now it was Rachel, not Tina, who was involved with Jason. And while Tina hadn't exactly waved a green flag, it also helped to know he was the only car on the course at the moment. He had the feeling there would be stop signs and detours, but he was determined that sooner or later he'd encounter a yield sign.

He hoped like hell it was sooner.

"So what do you think?" Ian asked over the hum of noise as he sat in the chair across from Reid. "Nice place, huh?"

Reid nodded. "And we're here because…?"

"Sophia invited us." Ian gestured to the waitress that he'd have the same as Reid.

The bottle of beer in Reid's hand paused halfway to his mouth. "Sophia Alexander?"

Ian grinned. "You know, the sister of the woman who's 'not on the menu,' as you put it."

"When did you talk to Sophia?"

"I called her today to see if she was busy tonight. She said she was coming here and suggested I stop by."

"You said she invited *us*."

"She's bringing Tina." Ian's grin widened. "Ah. I thought that might get your attention."

It more than got his attention. Carefully Reid set the bottle back down on the gray marble tabletop and scanned the room. He didn't see Tina or Sophia at a table or on the dance floor. Scanning the crowd again, he spotted Rachel walking into the room through an exit door behind the stage. Sophia came next.

Then Tina.

The black, Mandarin collar dress she wore emphasized her long neck and heart-shaped face. The knee-length hemline was conservative, the short sleeves demure. Nothing that should make his pulse jump or his mind stutter.

And yet it did—*she* did.

Keeping his gaze on Tina, he watched the sisters hurry to a front-row-center table as the dj announced that Controversy, the performing band for the evening, would be out in five.

Controversy. That was Jason's band, Reid remembered. So that's why Tina was here. Lifting the bottle of beer, Reid took a long pull, then sat back and waited for the show to begin.

"Stop fidgeting and relax." Tina handed Rachel a glass of ice water. "And breathe, for heaven's sake. It won't help Jason if you're passed out on the floor."

"You're right. I know, I'm sorry," Rachel said in a rush and sipped at the water. "But did you see him? Did you see how handsome he looks in his black satin jacket? And his hair, all that wonderful blond hair, loose around his shoulders."

"I saw him," Tina said. They'd just come from backstage where the band was waiting to come out. "He looked very handsome."

When the lights dimmed, Rachel turned white. "Oh, God, I think I'm going to be sick."

Rolling her eyes, Sophia dipped her fingers into the ice water, then flicked Rachel's face.

Rachel gasped, then scowled at Sophia. "Hey!"

"Got you breathing, didn't I? Now be quiet, sit still and let's see what your man can do."

But even Tina held her breath when the dj announced the band. Five men strolled out, everyone wearing sunglasses, looking very cool and very hot at the same time. They took their places, paused a moment, then the drummer tapped his drumsticks and said, "One, two, three, four!"

The lead guitar started solo, strong and loud, the drums rolled in a moment later. The sound was hard-beating southern blues. Like a living, breathing entity, the heavy bass and keyboard joined in, pulsating through the crowd, pulling them to their feet and moving them to the dance floor.

Then Jason stepped to the microphone.

"Tell me why…"

His voice trembled through the room, a smoky, raspy sound that was uniquely his own. A sound that echoed a hundred years of soul and sorrow, all the life of every blues singer who'd stepped on that stage before him. He sang of deception and lies, lost love and heartache. Passion flowed like lava from his words and set the room on fire.

This was Jason? Tina thought in stunned amazement. She'd never heard him sing before, had never dreamed he was this good. The audience and dancers moved to the beat, and Tina couldn't stop herself from moving with them. He was better than good, she thought. He was terrific.

Tina glanced at Rachel, saw the love shining in her eyes, and felt her chest swell with happiness for her sister. To be that deeply in love with someone, and to have them love you back, was a dream come true. Of course, in this case, the dream came with a few difficulties. But surely, Tina thought, when two people were that deeply in love, there was no difficulty that couldn't be resolved.

Tina could only hope that someday she'd find that kind of love, too. That someday there'd be a man who'd look at her the way Jason looked at Rachel.

Remembering Reid's kiss yesterday and the way he'd looked at her made Tina's stomach flutter. She knew it was just physical between them, but that didn't seem to discourage her thinking about the man constantly. If anything, it simply fueled the fire he'd lit inside her. Made her wonder what it would be like if he'd done more than kiss her, more than lightly brush his hands against her breasts. Her breasts ached just thinking about it, her skin felt tight and hot, and—

The room exploded with applause and cheers at the end of the band's first song. Thank goodness, Tina thought, shaking off the tingling sensation that had been curling through her blood. That kind of thinking was only going to lead to more sleepless nights.

While the applause continued, Rachel grabbed Tina's hand and squeezed. To say that Controversy had been well received was a bit of an understatement.

''Isn't he wonderful?'' Rachel shrieked over the noise. ''Isn't he?''

Laughing, Tina and Sophia hugged Rachel, then Sophia said, "I have to go say hi to someone. I'll be back in a little while."

Jason started his next song, a slower, soulful tale of forbidden love. Couples melted together on the dance floor, swaying gently to the music. Tears in her eyes, Rachel leaned forward in her chair and kept her eyes on Jason. Why he hadn't received a recording deal already amazed Tina, but she knew it was a tough business, that even the most talented singers and groups were often passed by. She hoped this would be Jason's chance to make his dream come true.

At the touch of a hand on her shoulder, Tina glanced up. A man flashed dimples and a diamond earring stud. His build was lean, his biceps the size of tree trunks. He nodded toward the dance floor.

She hesitated, though for the life of her, she didn't know why. She was at a club, for heaven's sake. A nice-looking man was standing here asking her to dance. Didn't she tell herself she was going to cut loose and have a good time?

So why was she so...uninterested? "Uh—"

"Sorry, pal, she's with me."

At the sound of the deep, familiar voice, Tina snapped her head around.

Reid?

Maybe this wasn't her lucky night, after all.

She watched the man who'd asked her to dance move away. Frowning, she looked back at Reid.

"I am not with you, and that was very pushy." She sipped from her water glass, wishing it were the wine she'd passed on earlier. "Maybe I wanted to dance with that man."

"Did you?"

Oh, why pretend? She was a lousy liar, and coy simply wasn't her style. She shrugged. "Not really."

Grinning, he sat in the chair Sophia had vacated. "Hi, Rachel."

"Hi, Reid," Rachel replied without taking her gaze off Jason. She had a dreamy, faraway look in her eyes.

"The wine you ordered, Mr. Danforth." A cocktail waitress set a bottle of wine and three glasses on the table, then filled the glasses. "Can I get you anything else?"

Tina didn't miss the suggestive tone in the waitress's voice. Or the lack of response from Reid when he shook his head.

"What are you doing here?" she asked him when he handed her a glass of wine.

"Same as you, watching the show."

She lifted a dubious brow. "Why do I have the feeling there's more?"

Reid slid a second glass of wine across the tabletop to Rachel, who didn't notice. "Sophia invited Ian."

"Really." Why did he have to look so handsome in his black leather blazer and sage-green T-shirt? And why did her pulse have to do somersaults every time she saw him? Gathering her wits, forcing her hand to stay steady, she took a sip of the wine. "And you just happened to come along?"

"Actually, Sophia told Ian to bring me."

Wine nearly sloshed out of her glass when her hand wobbled. My own flesh and blood conspiring against me. Wondering where her dear sister had disappeared to, Tina scanned the crowd, then spotted Sophia standing with Ian at the back of the room. When Sophia waggled her fingers and smiled knowingly, Tina glared back.

The band slipped into another fast number, and with the music so loud, it was easy to avoid any kind of serious conversation for the next few minutes. What she couldn't avoid or ignore was the proximity of Reid's body. His aftershave was woodsy, masculine, and she resisted the animal urge to slide closer and draw the intoxicating scent into her lungs.

When the music shifted back to a slow number, he leaned in, making her heart skip when he brought his mouth to her ear.

"With a voice like that," Reid said, nodding at Jason, "why's he working in a bakery?"

"The hours leave his afternoons and evenings free for writing and practicing with his band." His warm breath on her ear made it hard to think. "Mostly, he stays because of Rachel. They can see each other every day, and manage to sneak in a little private time, too, especially when my mother's not there."

"So your parents really don't know what's going on?"

Tina shook her head. "My father's kitchen is his own little world, and my mother—" she sipped at her wine, then shrugged "—well, her vision is skewed by her aspirations."

"What aspirations are those?"

With the wine cooling her nerves and Reid's voice warming her insides, Tina felt herself relaxing. "To see Sophia and Rachel married into prominence and wealth, and at least one grandbaby on the way. That's the real reason she bumped my restaurant and rented the space to your family. She sees the campaign headquarters as a hunting ground for potential husbands.''

''What about you?'' Reid asked. ''Doesn't she want to see you married, too?''

''Heavens, no.'' The laugh in her throat quickly faded when she realized that if she moved just a smidgen, Reid's mouth would be touching her neck. The very thought of it made her shiver and inch away. ''It doesn't matter that I'm twenty-four. I'm her baby. She doesn't think of me that way.''

He shook his head slowly. ''You're no baby, Tina.''

Something in Reid's voice, in his eyes, something dark and smoldering, sent heat pulsing through her veins. Was this a game to him? she wondered. And if it was, did she want to play? It would be dangerous and very foolish and she'd lose. She hadn't the experience or the skill to take on a man like Reid.

She'd be the one left hurting, she was certain of that. Was that a chance she could take?

Before she could even consider her answer, he'd already tugged her to her feet and was pulling her toward the dance floor. And when he drew her into his arms, she wasn't thinking at all.

The song was slow, smooth, as sexy as it was soulful. Her body molded to Reid's, and they moved as one. They were close, a blending of soft against hard. Even if she'd wanted to, she couldn't have pulled away. She cursed the fact that she didn't want to. She could have stood like this forever with Reid, her head on his shoulder, his arms tightly around her.

But there was no forever, not with Reid and not with

the song. When it ended, she sighed and lifted her head.

"Come home with me."

Her breath caught at his words. Her heart drummed. *Come home with me.* It would be so simple to leave here with him. To fall into his bed. She was certain it would be a night to remember.

But nothing would be simple tomorrow. She was just as certain about that, too.

While the dance floor began to clear and the band left the stage for a break, she imagined what it would be like. No man had ever made her feel like this before. Made her hot and cold at the same time. Made her ache. Made her yearn.

She needed space. Standing here, with Reid still holding her, she couldn't breathe, let alone think.

"Rachel is..."

"Backstage with Jason."

Tina glanced at the table where they'd all been sitting. The seats were all empty now. "Reid, I—"

He dipped his head, brushed his lips over hers. She forgot what she'd been about to say.

"I...I need a minute," she said breathlessly, shivered when he touched her cheek with his hand.

"I'll wait for you at the table."

Nodding, she turned, and on weak knees headed for the ladies' room. What kind of spell had he woven over her? she wondered. Whatever it was, it was as potent as it was formidable. A heady mix of excitement and fear.

Anticipation shivered through her.

Inside the rest room, Tina squeezed her way through

the mass of buzzing females and made her way to a sink. Dampening a paper towel, she pressed it to her cheeks and neck while the women around her slicked on fresh lipstick, smoothed their hair and adjusted their low-cut dresses and tops.

She looked at her own dress, and though it was pretty and she thought she looked nice enough, she still felt like a sparrow in the midst of swans. A daisy next to roses. For the hundredth time she wondered why Reid would want her. Even if all he wanted was a one-night stand, he had his pick of the most beautiful women in Savannah. For that matter, in the world. It simply made no sense to her.

But did it have to?

For once, did she have to be so damn logical, so sensible? she asked herself. While the women chattered and laughed and pressed all around her, Tina stared at her own reflection, not even certain who she was anymore. For once, couldn't she just let herself *be?* Let herself *feel?* Just enjoy the moment, the night, and not worry so much about tomorrow?

She felt a hand on her arm and blinked.

"Tina," Rachel said, her voice quavering. "We have to go."

"What?" When tears spilled from Rachel's eyes, Tina quickly pulled her sister into a stall and closed the door. "Rachel, honey, what's wrong?"

"We have to go. Please."

"What's happened? Are you all right?"

"I—" Rachel swallowed, then choked on a sob. "I broke up with Jason."

Six

He sat at the bar, nursing a beer, but he wasn't drunk. Not yet, anyway. At 2:00 a.m., the night was still young.

Reid figured he wasn't the first man to close down a bar thinking about a woman, and was even more certain he wouldn't be the last. In the ongoing battle between the sexes, womankind would forever remain a confusing and incredibly frustrating creature.

Reid decided that no woman could possibly be more confusing, or more frustrating, than Tina Alexander.

"Mind if I join you?"

Reid swiveled a glance at Jason. If the singer's face dropped any lower, it would be scraping the wood floor. After two encores his group had finished a few minutes ago. The club was starting to thin out, and even Ian had left after the music ended. But there were still plenty of late-nighters scattered in the bar. "You buying?"

"Sure." Jason slid onto the stool beside Reid, then gestured to the bartender for a new round.

"That was a hell of a performance."

"A record producer was in the audience." Based on Jason's tone, he might as well have said his best friend had died. "He wants the group to come to Los Angeles next week and cut a demo."

"Congratulations."

Jason shrugged, took a long pull from the beer bottle that appeared in front of him. "I asked Rachel to come with me."

Reid waited, didn't think he needed to ask the obvious question.

"She broke it off." Jason dragged a hand through his hair. "Told me she was happy for me, but she didn't want to see me anymore. She asked me if we could just be friends. Friends, for God sakes! Why the hell would she say something like that?"

Reid shook his head. As if he had any answers when it came to women. But he realized it just might explain why Tina had left without even saying goodbye.

When she hadn't come back from the rest room, he'd assumed she'd made up her mind about coming home with him and the answer had been no. He'd also considered it might be payback for the way he'd left her in the garden the night before. Somehow, though, he didn't think that was Tina's style, and when Rachel hadn't come back, either, even after the band started playing again, and Sophia seemed to disappear, as well, it hadn't taken a rocket scientist to figure out something was up. Now he at least had an inkling why the Alexander women had all vanished like smoke in the wind.

His expression dark, Jason looked at Reid. "I wanted to put a fist in your face. Nearly jumped off the stage a couple of times. You're bigger than me, but I figured the element of surprise would be in my favor, in the short run, anyway."

Reid lifted a brow. "What did I do?"

Jason shrugged. "I see you sitting with my girl, then she breaks up with me. What would you think if you saw the woman you love with another guy?"

"I have no idea," Reid said honestly. "I've never been in love."

"Lucky you." Jason shook his head. "It hurts like hell. Walking around with your heart on your sleeve, it's damn embarrassing."

Reid might have agreed, but why kick a guy when he was down? And anyway, if that's what love felt like, he wanted no part of it.

"Anyway—" Jason sighed "—once I calmed down a little, I figured out she didn't break up with me because of you. I've just been jealous since you showed up. Everyone's talking about seeing you and Rachel together, and what a great pair you'd make. I know she wouldn't cheat on me, but the thought of you making a move on her made me crazy."

"Women do that to a man," Reid said with nod.

They clinked bottles and drank.

"All Mariska talks about is having a Danforth for a son-in-law." Anger narrowed Jason's eyes. "How's that supposed to make a guy feel?"

Not so good, Reid figured. Unless the guy happened to be a Danforth and had a thing for one of Mariska's daughters. Not that he was interested in marriage, of course, Reid thought. Hell, no. Maybe one day he'd settle down, but that was way in the future. He was attracted to Tina, very attracted, but he sure wasn't ready for picket fences and baby carriages.

When Jason indicated another round to the bartender, Reid could see that an already long night was going to be even longer. What the hell, he thought with a sigh. There were taxis outside and he didn't have any better place to be, anyway. He'd pay for it in the morning, as would Jason, but somehow getting drunk tonight seemed to beat the alternative of being alone.

"If I live to be a hundred, I'll never love again." Her nose red, her eyes swollen from her tears, Rachel stared unseeing at the cup of peppermint tea that Tina set on the kitchen table. "My life is over."

After two pots of coffee, and because it was nearly three in the morning, Tina had brewed a pot of organic tea. With all the caffeine buzzing in her system, she doubted she'd be able to fall asleep for three days. In the corner, Delilah slept peacefully in her cushioned basket.

"Your life is not over," Tina said. "We'll figure something out."

Rachel shook her head. "The minute he told me he was going to Los Angeles, I knew we had to break up. He's going to be a star, Tina. A big star. I'd only be in his way."

Tina sighed. They'd been over this a hundred times since they'd left Steam, but Rachel was being ridiculously stubborn. "He loves you, Rachel. You know he does."

"Did you see the way all those women were looking at him tonight?" She reached for another tissue from the nearly empty box on the table. "Why would he stay with me, subject himself to all the hassels from Mom and Dad, when he could have any woman he wants?"

"He wants *you,* Ray." Tina couldn't understand why her sister had suddenly become so incredibly unreasonable and emotional. "He adores you. Don't give up so easily. We'll call Jason tomorrow."

"And you." Delicately Rachel blew her nose. "I ruined your night, too. You should have gone back to the club with Sophia."

"For one thing, I only went there for you," Tina said firmly. It killed her to see Rachel like this, frustrated her that she couldn't talk any sense into her. "And for another thing, do you think I'd leave you alone when you're hurting like this? If Sophia hadn't already promised the owner she'd help him close tonight, she wouldn't have gone back, either."

"Still, if it wasn't for me," Rachel said forlornly, "you'd be with Reid right now."

Tina's pulse jumped. "What are you talking about?"

"For heaven's sake." Rachel rolled her reddened eyes. "I'm not blind. I saw the way he was looking at you."

Hoping her hand wouldn't shake, Tina calmly picked up her cup of tea. "What way was that?"

"Like he wanted to cover you with whipped cream and lick it all off."

"Rachel!" Tea sloshed out of Tina's cup. "You didn't just say that!"

A smile, the first one since they'd left the club, curved Rachel's lips. "Why shouldn't I say it? It's true, isn't it?"

Reaching for a napkin, Tina wiped up the spilled tea. "He looks at every woman that way."

"He never looked at me that way, or Sophia." Rachel pulled her feet up onto the chair and wrapped her arms around her knees. "And *every* man looks at Sophia that way. So did he ask you?"

"Ask me what?"

"To spend the night with him."

"Rachel!" Tina's cup clattered onto its saucer.

"Stop saying my name." Rachel dropped her chin on her knees. "Besides, it makes me feel better to talk about your love life. You want me to feel better, don't you?"

"Okay, okay." Tina rolled her head back. "So he asked me. But I assure you, it has nothing to do with love."

"I knew it." Rachel hugged her legs tighter. "So what did you say?"

"I never exactly got around to answering."

"And then I pulled you away," Rachel said on a sigh. "Oh, T, I'm so sorry. To think you've had to sit here all night and listen to my problems, when you could have had a glorious night making love with Reid Danforth.''

"Sex." Her tea had a bitter taste when she swallowed. "Nothing more than that. You saved me from a big mistake."

"You don't know that." Rachel covered Tina's hand with her own. "I saw you two dancing together. There was something there, T. Something more than just sex."

If only that were true, she thought. But she couldn't let herself believe that, couldn't let herself even think it. If she did, she'd be the one sitting here with red eyes and a broken heart, emptying a box of tissues.

Shaking her head, Tina smiled at her sister. "It's for the best, Ray. Reid and I just aren't meant to—"

A scuffling from the stairwell outside had both women turning.

"Rachel! Open up." A loud knock rattled the front door. "I know you're in there. Open up this door."

"Jason!" Rachel's eyes widened in horror. "Ohmigod, Tina, don't tell him I'm here. Please!"

The pounding continued, and despite her sister's pleas, Tina rose and headed for the door. "You're going to have to face him sometime, honey. It might as well be now."

"No, Tina, I can't." Rachel followed, pulling on Tina's arm. "I'm not ready. Maybe tomorrow."

"It *is* tomorrow," Tina said and opened the door, prepared to face a lovesick Jason.

At the sight of Reid standing on the doorstep holding up an obviously inebriated Jason, Tina's heart slammed in her chest.

"Sorry." Reid's smile was apologetic. "He was insistent."

Rachel rushed past Tina and threw her arms around Jason. "Jason, oh, sweetie, what have you done?"

"Rachel, sugar, I love you." Clumsily, Jason reached for Rachel. "I won't go to L.A., baby. I won't go anywhere without you. Come here and kiss me."

"You idiot." But she did kiss him. "You big fat idiot. I'll take you home."

While Rachel slipped her heels back on and tugged on her coat, Reid held Jason on his feet. When he started to sing to her, Rachel's eyes filled with tears and she kissed him again. Tina shifted awkwardly and met Reid's gaze. He simply grinned.

"I'll help you downstairs," Reid said to Rachel when she managed to pull her lips from Jason's.

She shook her head. "Thanks, we'll be all right."

"That's right, baby," Jason mumbled, kissing Rachel's neck. "We'll be all right."

Arms around each other, they stumbled out the door, closing it behind them.

"Well." Tina let out a long breath when it was quiet again. "You want to tell me how you two ended up together?"

With a shrug, Reid slipped his hands into his pockets. "Guess he needed someone to talk to."

She couldn't imagine a more unlikely coalition. "No offense, Reid, but Jason doesn't like you."

"Only because he thought I was interested in Rachel." He leveled his gaze on hers as he slipped off his jacket. "Now that he knows it's you I want, we're pals."

His words thrilled her, made her pulse leap and her skin heat up. When he tossed his jacket on the sofa and moved close, her throat turned to dust. "Reid, I…this is not a good idea."

"Maybe not."

"We barely know each other."

He nodded. "You're absolutely right."

"We should just say good-night now."

"Probably."

"Oh, for heaven's sake." Fisting her hands in the front of his shirt, she yanked him close. "Must you be so damn agreeable?"

Smiling, his arms came around her. "I aim to please."

And he did please, she thought dimly when his mouth covered hers. Senses reeling, she melted against his strong chest, slid her arms up his broad shoulders. When he deepened the kiss, she met the thrust of his tongue with her own, and the minty, hot taste of him made her knees weak and her toes curl.

She could stop this, she *should* stop, but she didn't want to. Since the day she'd met Reid they'd been moving toward this moment like a runaway train. They were careening out of control and it was as exhilarating as it was exciting. All she could do was hold on for the ride; she knew it would be a wild one.

She squirmed against him, anticipation vibrating through her. She'd waited so long—a lifetime—for this moment. Now that it was here, impatience had her clutching at his shoulders, moaning. She wanted to remember every moment, every thrilling touch, every glorious taste.

His breath was as ragged as her own; she could feel the heavy beat of his heart against her aching breasts. How she wanted him to touch her there, she thought. And other places. And how she wanted to touch him, too. Her hands, her fingers itched to explore his body.

He dragged his mouth from hers, his midnight-blue gaze seared her to the core. ''Bedroom,'' he managed, but was kissing her again before she could answer.

Slowly but steadily, their bodies still molded to each other, their mouths still fused, they inched their way across the living room, through the hall. So far, she thought, so incredibly far...

Had he ever wanted a women like this? Reid wondered while they made that long journey to the bedroom. If he had, that woman, that moment was lost to him forever. There was just here and now and Tina.

It had required tremendous willpower not to take her right there on the living room floor. Only the thought that he might hurt her had him reining in the raw need clutching at his gut. If it killed him, he'd take his time with her. Slow, he told himself. He'd take it slow. He wanted her underneath him, writhing with need, pleading, and just the thought of it nearly made him lose it before they'd even stepped into the bedroom.

He trailed kisses down her neck, reveled in the soft sounds she made deep in her throat. When he nipped at her earlobe, she shivered.

''So sweet,'' he murmured.

They moved through the doorway, into the bedroom.

Soft light shone from a beaded lamp on a nightstand, shimmered through drops of clear crystals and reflected on the walls. Pillows of all shapes and sizes adorned the deep-green comforter on the large, four-poster bed. The faint smell of lavender hung in the air, mixed with the heady scent of desire.

Standing next to the bed, he lifted his head, gazed down at her. Her lashes fluttered open, and her eyes, glazed with passion, met his.

Keeping his gaze on hers, he reached for the embroidered closure at the base of her neck, flicked it open, then slid his hand underneath. He felt the wild beating of her heart under his fingertips, the warmth of her bare skin, then slid the soft fabric off one creamy-white shoulder. He pressed his mouth to the curve of her neck and nibbled. On a soft purr, her head rolled back.

Tina wondered how she would survive the sensations consuming her. She felt as if every nerve, every cell, were exposed, a pleasure so intense it bordered on pain. Heat pumped through her veins, a rushing, hot river of need. Dizzy, she swayed against him, and the intimate press of her body against his startled yet thrilled her at the same time.

While his arms held her steady, his lips moved down her neck to nuzzle her shoulder. The light scrape of his teeth, the hot slide of his tongue over her skin made her whimper. She wanted that mouth on her, she realized, wanted his mouth and his hands everywhere.

As if he'd read her mind, he slipped both hands under the loosened neckline of her dress and slid the garment completely off her shoulders, then down her arms to her waist.

"Sexy," he murmured when his gaze dropped to her skimpy black lace bra.

The flicker of shyness she felt dissolved when she saw the dark, intense look of need in his eyes. When he cupped her breasts in his large hands and lightly kneaded, she drew in a deep breath. When he brought his mouth to her lace-covered nipple and suckled the beaded tip with his hot lips, she gasped.

Burrowing her fingers into his hair, she arched upward, clutching at him. A meteor of white-hot pleasure streaked from her breast to the ache between her legs. The need she felt turned to a burning throb.

"Reid," she whispered, not even recognizing the sound of her own voice. She had no idea who this wanton stranger was who had invaded her body, but she welcomed the intruder with open arms. She'd never felt so alive in her entire life. So aware. The smooth texture of Reid's hair between her fingers, the masculine scent of his skin, the ragged sound of his breathing. There were colors and textures behind her eyes, and wonderful, ever-changing shapes and images.

While he moved his attention to her other breast, his hands guided her dress down her hips. The fabric pooled at her bare feet. She squirmed, wanting him with a desperation that was driving her mad. When he lifted his head, circled her waist with his hands and brought his mouth to her stomach, she moaned.

"So pretty," he murmured, sliding his mouth across the bottom of her rib cage. "So delicate."

His mouth and words aroused her even more and the urgency grew. As he trailed hot kisses across her belly, her hands pressed against his skull. She didn't think she could take much more; she was certain a person could die from feelings this intense.

"Reid," she whispered hoarsely. "Please."

She helped him drag his top over his head. Wanting desperately to touch him, she reached out and slid her hands over the hard muscles of his shoulders and chest, felt the raw power and strength under her fingertips. When she leaned closer and pressed her mouth to his collarbone, he sucked in a sharp breath.

His taste, salty and warm, intoxicated her. She felt his heart pounding under her fingertips, felt the coiled energy rippling through his muscles. *Mine,* she thought. Even if only for this one night, he was really hers.

And she was his.

He lowered her to the bed, and the weight of his body pressed her into the soft mattress. He crushed his mouth to hers, demanding, insistent. She quivered when his hand found her breast again, arched upward when his mouth replaced his hand.

Every touch, every taste, every sensation, each one more intense than the one before, rolled through her, building and building. She wanted, needed, him inside her. Needed to end this incredible, wonderful torture. But when his hand slid down her stomach, then slipped under her lace panties and dipped to the pebbled heat between her legs, she knew the exquisite torture had only just begun. He stroked her, matching the rhythm of his tongue against her own. She moved with him, frustrated at the pace he had set. Determined to speed things up, she slid her hands between them and loosened his belt, then reached for the zipper of his slacks.

Every thought of going slowly raced out of Reid's mind when Tina closed her hand around him. He knew she was ready for him; she was wet and swollen, arching her body to his. With the last thread of control, he moved away from her.

"Reid." She whimpered in protest and reached for him.

"Don't worry, sweetheart, I'm not going anywhere." While he tugged off the rest of his clothes and took the extra moment to protect them both, he kept his gaze locked with hers.

Her eager arms welcomed him back. He kissed her deeply, tenderly, let the passion rise to the same fever pitch before he slipped her panties off, then moved between her thighs. She opened to him, wrapped her long, silky legs around him and pulled him into her.

When she stiffened and softly cried out, he went still.

"What…?"

Her arms and legs tightened around him, held him close. "Don't stop," she said raggedly. "Please, Reid."

"But you…but I—"

She reared up, kissing him, moving her hips against him, making it impossible for him to think, impossible to do anything but hang on to the growing wave of sheer, raw need. Helpless, he moved inside the tight, hot velvet glove of her body. Blind pleasure, dark and uncontrollable, took over. The wave rose, then rose higher still, until it finally crested. She hovered there, shuddering, a moan on her lips.

His own climax slammed violently into him and broke apart, crashed and rolled.

Lungs burning, he pulled her close while his mind struggled to pull words into a coherent sentence.

"Tina." His voice was raspy, strained. "Why didn't you tell me?"

While her hand moved restlessly over his chest, she snuggled in his arms. "I didn't think about it."

"You didn't think about it?" His voice cracked. "How could you not think about it?"

"I was a little busy." Her hand stilled. "Would it have made a difference if I'd told you I was a virgin?"

"Yes. No." He jerked a hand through his hair. "Yes."

"I'm twenty-four years old, Reid," she said thinly. "I waited to be with a man until it felt right to me. I'm sorry if that's a problem for you."

When she started to move away, he hauled her back and pressed a kiss to her temple.

"I didn't say it was a problem. I just would have been more careful," he said quietly. "I hurt you."

Slowly she relaxed, then shook her head. "A twinge, that's all, just for a moment. Everything else was wonderful. You were wonderful."

"Yeah? How wonderful?"

"Oh, stop grinning at me like that." She pushed at his chest. "As if you don't hear that all the time."

He rose on one elbow and frowned at her. "What's that supposed to mean?"

"I've seen your name in magazines and newspapers,'' she said with a timid shrug. ''There's usually a woman's name attached somewhere.''

''Don't believe everything you read, sweetheart.'' He gathered her close again and lay back on the bed. ''I've dated a lot of women, had a few I'd even call girlfriends. I may not be a saint, but I sure as hell didn't sleep with them all, either. Okay?''

Silence settled around them like a soft blanket. Somewhere in the room a clock tick-tocked; warm air hummed through an overhead duct.

''Why me?'' she asked quietly, stroking her fingertips back and forth across his chest.

Would this woman ever stop surprising him? he wondered. Strangely, he realized that was part of the attraction.

Because the way she was touching him was a big distraction, he took hold of her hand, then hauled her on top of him. She gasped at the unexpected movement, and the fact that he was hard and ready for her again, wanting her as much now as he had only a few minutes ago.

''You really don't know, do you?'' He was definitely enjoying the new position of her body on top of his, not to mention the view of her bare breasts. ''You really are completely unaware of how sexy and utterly captivating you are.''

Her cheeks turned pink and her lashes fluttered down. ''I figured you were just bored.''

''Bored?'' He nearly choked. ''Good Lord, woman. Where would you get an idea like that?''

''Sharie Jo Sullivan.''

''Who?''

"Sharie Jo Sullivan. A customer at the bakery. She said men like you get bored easily. That you're always looking for a challenge."

"Is that what you think you are to me?" He couldn't believe he was hearing this. "A challenge?"

"I was probably the first woman who ever said no to you," she reminded him.

"I didn't hear you say no tonight." Reid skimmed his hands down Tina's back, then brought his mouth to hers and nibbled one delicious corner. "In fact, I believe I heard a lot of 'yes' and 'please,'" he teased.

"You're going to need a new head to fit that ego if you aren't careful, buster," she said with a prim sniff.

"I'll be careful." He cupped her firm behind, watched her eyes widen when he moved his hips against hers. "Very careful."

"Darn you, Reid Danforth. You've turned me into a loose woman." Lifting her hips, she took him inside her. "Remind me later to thank you."

Later turned out to be close to ten in the morning, with food the motivating force that finally pulled them out of the bedroom. While Reid showered, Tina had her omelettes cooking and her own special recipe of breakfast potatoes warming in the oven. Considering the night they'd had, she was certain he was going to be one hungry man.

Lord knew, she thought with a smile, he certainly was a man with an appetite.

They'd dozed on and off throughout the early morning hours, waking briefly enough for a kiss or a touch...sometimes more. Remembering how eager she'd been for him brought a blush to her cheeks. And though she had no idea what today, tomorrow or next week would bring for her, she had no regrets at all. She'd waited twenty-four years for last night, and even now, in the light of day, she was so glad.

It had been amazing. *He* had been amazing. But there'd been no whispered promises, no mention of the future, and though it pained her to think that last night might be their only night together, she'd gone to him with her eyes wide open.

Unfortunately, her heart had been wide open, as well.

Sometime during the night, or maybe the first time she'd laid eyes on him, she realized, she'd fallen in love with Reid. She'd fought it, of course. It was, after all, very foolish and completely reckless. But clearly, reason did not prevail when it came to love. It simply was.

At the sound of the shower turning off, she slipped her omelettes onto plates, loaded on potatoes and was setting them on the table when he walked into the kitchen wearing nothing but a knotted towel slung low on his hips. Her heart jumped at the sight, and that ache she'd become so familiar with last night pulsed through her veins. The intensity of it startled her, had her wondering, and worrying, about tomorrow.

She couldn't think about that now, refused to let herself give in to fear. She would accept what they had and be happy for it.

And then he smiled at her and her heart shattered.

"Hey."

"Hey, yourself." She swallowed the lump in her

throat and forced herself to smile back. "Breakfast is ready."

"Smells great."

He walked toward her, made every piece of her heart vibrate with longing.

"It'll be on the breakfast menu of my restaurant in one year." She hoped her voice sounded as easy as she intended. "As soon as I have my space back from you, of course."

When he moved beside her and leaned close, her breath held, waiting for his kiss. But he reached past her to the table and snatched a slice of potato instead, then popped it in his mouth.

"Tasty."

"Thanks."

She was about to turn when he tugged her to him, then covered her mouth with his. She melted into the kiss, felt it sing through her entire body.

"Very tasty," he murmured against her lips and pulled her closer. "You know what they say, don't you?"

"What?" she whispered, sliding her arms around his neck.

"If you can't stand the heat—" he scooped her up in his arms "—get out of the kitchen."

Laughing, she wrapped her arms around him and held on as he headed for the bedroom. At the sound of keys jangling in the doorknob, Reid stopped and turned. Tina froze, watched in horror as the door swung open.

"Well, now, what have we here?"

Ohmigod.

Clutching her robe together across her bared breasts, Tina blinked, then sucked in a lungful of air and managed a weak smile. "Hi, Aunt Yana."

Seven

Aunt Yana? Reid glanced at the photo of Tina's aunt hanging on the wall, then back at the woman standing in the doorway. Yep. Aunt Yana, all right.

She wore a deep-blue, long, flowing duster over silk ivory pants. Colorful stones dangled from her ears and circled a long, slender neck. In spite of the incredibly awkward moment, it was impossible for Reid not to be stunned by the older woman's beauty. A short crop of thick, straight sable-brown hair accented high cheekbones, aristocratic nose and gypsy-green eyes.

Her mouth, wide and full, slowly curved up at the corners as she closed the door behind her.

"You...you're home early," Tina sputtered.

"My shoot finished ahead of schedule." Yana slid a large straw handbag from her shoulder and dropped it on the entry table along with her keys, slid her gaze from the tip of Reid's bare toes to the towel draping his hips, then up to his face. "Aren't you going to introduce me to your friend, Katina?"

"I—oh, of course." Tina gulped. "This is Reid Danforth. Reid, my aunt, Yana Alexander Dimetri Romano."

Not quite certain what the proper etiquette was for the situation, Reid simply nodded. "A pleasure, Ms. Romano."

"I think just Yana would be more appropriate." Folding her arms, Yana glanced back down at the towel. Amusement danced in her eyes. "All things considered."

"Yes, ma'am."

"Reid," Tina whispered, her voice strained. "Could you, ah, put me down?"

"Oh. Right."

When her feet touched the floor, Tina tightened the belt of her robe. Her face had gone from pale to rosy pink. "We were just…ah, going to have breakfast."

"Of course you were." Yana's smile widened. "It smells wonderful."

"I'll set another plate." Tina shifted from one bare foot to the other. "Just give me…us, a minute, to ah—"

"I believe I hear something buzzing." Yana glanced at the sport coat lying on the sofa, then looked back at Reid. Though the sound was faint, it was definitely a buzz. "Yours, I assume?"

He'd have to kill whoever was calling him, Reid decided. Holding tightly to the knot of the towel, he stepped to the sofa and retrieved his cell phone from his jacket.

"Excuse me." He backed toward the bedroom where he'd left his clothes.

"Take your time, dear," Yana called after him. "My niece and I could use a minute alone to say hello."

Closing the bedroom door behind him, Reid snapped the phone to his ear. "Yeah."

"Reid, where have you been? I've been trying to reach you all morning."

"Kimberly?" He heard the stress in his sister's voice. "Are you all right?"

"You have to come to Crofthaven right away. In the attic. They, they were working there this morning, and found—"

At the sound of her quiet sob, fear snaked through him. "Found what, Kim?"

"They found a body."

At least a dozen patrol cars were already at Crofthaven when Reid pulled in front of the mansion's main entrance. Several uniformed officers standing outside turned at the sight of the black BMW screeching to a halt, then quietly returned to their conversations after Reid hurried past them.

The first officers on the scene had carefully taken in every detail of the activities at Crofthaven. Later they would have the inside scoop to give to the rest of the station, not to mention their friends and family. And if they were really lucky, they just might find their faces on TV or in the newspapers.

The public, not to mention Abraham's rival candidates, would eat up every tasty morsel of the juicy story.

"Reid." Ian was coming down the stairs as Reid stepped into the foyer. "Thank God you're here."

"Tell me what's happened." Reid met his brother at the base of the stairs. "Kimberly called and said they found a body in the attic, but I didn't get much more out of her."

"She's pretty shook up." Ian dragged a hand through his hair and sighed. "Reid, we think it might be Victoria."

It was like taking a punch in the gut, and it was a moment before Reid could speak. "Vickie?"

"'Fraid so."

Victoria Danforth had suddenly disappeared five years ago and, though there'd been a nationwide hunt and several private detectives had been hired, no one had ever found a trace of their cousin.

"How is that possible?" Just the thought of it made Reid's stomach clench. "How could she be up there all this time? We searched everywhere."

"That section of the house has been closed up for years," Ian said. "And it also appears there was some kind of hidden compartment. If Dad hadn't decided to reopen that wing and renovate, we might not have ever found the body."

"Are they sure it's her?"

Ian shook his head. "The coroner's up there now, taking pictures and running a few preliminary tests. It could be days or even weeks before we have a positive ID."

At the sound of hushed voices, Reid glanced toward the living room. "Uncle Harold and Aunt Miranda?"

"They're in the living room with Dad and the rest of the family. If it is Vickie, they want to know as soon as possible."

All the years of not knowing if their daughter was alive or dead. He couldn't even imagine the agony his aunt and uncle had gone through. But even through their devastating loss, even as the months and years had passed without a trace of what had happened, they, and the entire family, hadn't given up hope that one day Vickie would be found alive.

And they wouldn't give up hope now, either, Reid thought somberly. Not until they had tangible, physical proof.

"What about the press?" Reid was surprised they weren't already swarming the mansion like locusts. "What do they know?"

"Nothing yet. Dad's called in a couple of favors to keep this quiet for a day or two, but I doubt we can contain it much longer. Nicola will put together a statement today."

"And the police?"

"They want to speak with the entire family," Ian said. "Right now they're questioning Joyce."

Reid frowned. "Why Joyce?"

"Procedure." Ian shrugged. "I guess they figure the housekeeper always knows everything, sees everything."

"That's certainly true with Joyce," Reid said with a nod. "When we were kids, I always swore that woman had eyes in the back of her head and superhero hearing.''

Ian furrowed his brow. ''Doesn't she?''

Reid managed a grin, then sighed. ''We might as well settle in with everyone else. Looks like it's going to be a long day.''

''Based on the fact you're still in the same clothes I saw you in last night—'' Ian took in his brother's rumpled appearance ''—it looks like your night was a long one, too. Want to tell me about it?''

''Not really.'' He wasn't ready to talk about Tina yet. Wasn't certain what his feelings were, though there was no question he had them. Stronger than any feelings he'd ever had for a woman before.

It was just as well that Tina's aunt had come in when she had, Reid thought. After the night they'd had, a little distance might be a good thing.

But even as Reid followed Ian to the living room, even as he told himself that his family needed him now, that there was a much bigger issue than anything happening in his own personal life, he still couldn't get Tina Alexander out of his mind.

''These potatoes are delicious.'' Yana speared a small slice and popped it in her mouth. ''Your creation?''

Freshly showered and dressed, Tina sat down at the kitchen table. It was just like her aunt to avoid the most obvious question and discuss something as innocuous as potatoes. ''Aunt Yana, I can explain—''

''I don't need the recipe.'' Yana waved her fork.

"You know I never cook unless I'm absolutely forced to."

Tina almost smiled. It was also like her aunt to make light of an awkward situation. "You know what I mean."

"I'm forty-eight years old, Katina," Yana said. "I've been married twice. There's very little you could explain to me that I don't already know."

Tina dropped her gaze. "I...I just don't want you to think that I was...that I—"

"Katina. Look at me." Yana slipped a finger under Tina's chin and lifted. "I was there the day you were born. Such a pretty baby, all pink and bright-eyed. Now you're a beautiful woman. All grown up."

Tina shook her head. "You have to say that. You're my aunt."

"I say it because it's true." Lovingly Yana touched Tina's cheek. "I can see you don't believe me, but one day you will."

She didn't believe her, of course, but still it felt good to hear the words. Tina smiled at her aunt, then said shyly, "It was my first time."

"You always were the cautious one," Yana said with a nod. "And I can see you are still being cautious. What is it you're afraid of, Katina?"

"I—" It was one thing to think it, Tina realized, but to say it out loud was quite another. She drew in a steadying breath. "I think I'm falling in love with him."

"And why is this such a bad thing?"

"I don't know how I'll survive when he...when it's over," she said quietly. "But just thinking about it makes my chest ache. I'm not sure I'm strong enough.''

"You're strong enough.'' Yana's expression was as patient as it was thoughtful. "But is he?''

Tina furrowed her brow. "What do you mean?''

"Never mind, my dear.'' Yana patted Tina's hand and smiled. "Now tell me, was he a good lover?''

Tina nearly choked, felt the heat of a blush race up her neck and across her cheeks. She couldn't believe she was sitting here having this conversation with her aunt. But then, she still couldn't believe that last night had really happened at all.

Smiling slowly, she met her aunt's eyes. "He was wonderful.''

"Nagyszeru," Yana said, smiling. "He is also very handsome. I would have liked to photograph him, especially in that towel.'' Her aunt's smile turned lusty. "Or without. Maybe you will ask him for me?''

Tina gasped at the outrageous request. But the thought of it also warmed her blood. She knew what that incredible body looked like firsthand, what it felt like against her own.

"Oh, Aunt Yana.'' Laughing, Tina threw her arms around her aunt and hugged her tightly. "I'm so glad you're here. Welcome home.''

Every Sunday Mariska spent most of her day cooking a six-course meal for her family while Ivan watched sports from his easy chair in the den. From the time they were tall enough to see over the kitchen counter, all of the Alexander daughters helped in the preparation. Though the menu varied, the tradition was strict. Attendance was mandatory, no excuses accepted.

Today was no exception.

"Your mother wants the good silverware and china tonight." Carrying the wooden box that contained the silver set, Yana came through the swinging kitchen door. "Are we celebrating something?"

"She wants the crystal candle holders, too," Tina said, smoothing the wrinkles from the white linen tablecloth. She and Yana had walked in the front door only minutes ago and there'd been no time to find out what was going on.

"Maybe it's because she won at bingo last night." Rachel pulled plates from the cherrywood buffet and set them on the table. "She made chicken paprika and has a bottle of Putonos chilling."

"She's definitely got something she's happy about." Yana handed the silverware box to Tina, then winked at both her nieces. "I'll go see if I can pry it out of her."

When Yana went back into the kitchen, Tina moved close to Rachel. It was the first time since she'd walked in the door that they'd been alone. "Are you all right?"

Rachel nodded. "I sneaked in late last night after Mom and Dad were asleep."

Shaking her head, Tina sighed. "We're too old for this, Ray. We've got to talk to Mom and Dad, both of us."

"I know, I know." Then Rachel's eyes widened. "Both of us? Are you saying what I think you're saying?"

"Yeah." Tina smiled slowly. "I am."

"What's going on?" Sophia swung through the door carrying the candlesticks. She looked at Tina, then Rachel. "No fair. You're telling secrets without me."

"Not me, Tina," Rachel whispered. "She and Reid—"

"Oh, heck—" waving a hand, Sophia moved next to her sisters and formed a circle "—tell me something I don't know."

Tina's jaw dropped. "How do you know?"

"I saw it on your face the minute you walked in, T. Your feet weren't even touching the floor."

"Don't be ridiculous." No one could tell something like that, Tina thought. Lord, she certainly hoped not. Shaking her head, she stepped away from her sisters and opened the silverware box. "But I will admit, it was a little interesting when Yana came home this morning and found Reid wearing nothing but a towel."

Gasping, Rachel clasped a hand to her chest and Sophia lifted a brow. When their father looked over at them from his easy chair, they all quickly turned their attention back to setting the table, then glanced up at each other and started to laugh.

Tina realized how important all this was to her. Family. Tradition. Sharing secrets with her sisters. She knew that no matter how much their lives might change, they would always be there for each other, all of them. Through thick and thin, through happy and sad. Tina could only pray that the happy times would be more plentiful than the sad.

They were nearly finished setting the table when Yana came back out of the kitchen carrying a marble trivet.

"Did you find out anything?" Tina asked.

"As a matter of fact, I did," Yana said. "Rachel, grab another plate and put it on the table, please, and another set of silverware, too."

"I already have six," Tina said, recounting to be sure.

"You'll need seven."

"Seven?"

When the doorbell rang, every head turned.

Yana smiled. "I'll get it."

Tina had a bad feeling as she watched her aunt walk across the living room. A bad, bad feeling.

When Yana opened the door, the bad feeling became a reality.

Reid.

He stood on the front step, the bouquet of roses in his hand bright pink, the dress shirt under his sport coat slate blue. Tina's heart stopped, then began to race.

"What's he doing here?" Rachel grabbed Tina's arm.

"I...I don't know."

Tina and Rachel and Sophia all looked at each other, then said at the same time, *"Mom."*

"Reid." With all the grace of a queen, Yana held out her hand. "What a pleasure to see you again."

"Ms. Romano." Reid handed the roses to Yana, who lifted them to her nose and breathed in their scent.

"How lovely. Please, come in. Mariska will be out in a moment."

"Thank you."

The house was open and warm, Reid noted as he stepped into the foyer of the living room. Beige walls, hardwood floors, a large burgundy sofa covered with tapestry pillows. Lots of framed family photos. The delicious scent of spices and chicken made his mouth water and reminded him he'd barely eaten anything since he'd left Tina at Yana's apartment that morning.

"Girls." Yana slipped her arm through Reid's. "Look who's here."

"Rachel, Sophia." When his gaze shifted to Tina, their eyes met and held. "Tina."

Lips softly parted in shock, she nodded back. It didn't take a genius to figure out that his visit had not been expected.

Though fewer than eight hours had passed since he'd seen her, it felt like days. He wanted to tell her how pretty she looked in a cardigan the same rosy blush as her cheeks and a simple black skirt, but he held himself in check. Knowing that he couldn't just walk up to her and kiss her, he shoved his hands into his pockets. "Reid!" Carrying a steaming casserole, Mariska burst out of the kitchen. "You are just in time."

"Thank you for inviting me, Mrs. Alexander."

"Please, you must call me Mariska," she reminded him. "I am so glad you could come at such short notice."

He glanced at Tina again, who was staring at her

mother in disbelief. "I assure you," Reid said with a smile, "it's my pleasure."

When Ivan yelled something rude from the other room, Mariska shook her head. "My husband and football. I have to pry him out of his chair if there is a game on."

Mariska set the casserole on the table, then frowned at her daughters. "Why do you all stand there like stones? Sophia, get our guest a drink. Yana, will you please tell your brother that supper is ready."

When Rachel started to move toward the kitchen, Mariska stopped her. "Rachel, you keep Reid company while Tina and I bring out the food."

"But—" Rachel cast a nervous glance at Tina, who shook her head "—all right."

When everyone scurried off, Reid leaned down and whispered, "Jason was great last night."

Rachel's nerves seemed to calm at the mention of Jason's name, and her eyes brightened. "Thank you for taking care of him."

While he and Rachel quietly talked about Jason and his band, Reid sipped on the glass of beer Sophia brought him and watched as dish after loaded dish of food came out of the kitchen. Wine and water glasses were filled, crisp white linen napkins were laid beside each plate.

Every time Tina came into the room, their eyes would meet. Every time she would blush, then hurry back out.

"Dinner is ready." Mariska came out of the kitchen carrying a platter of chicken. "Reid, you sit in the chair beside Rachel."

Reid was beginning to have an understanding of what Jason had been going through by needing to hide his feelings for Rachel. It was killing him, Reid thought as he pulled out Rachel's chair for her, that he couldn't touch Tina, or slip an arm around her waist, or even kiss her cheek. Though this might not be the right time, he was determined to make it clear— very soon—that it was Tina he wanted to be with, not Rachel.

Ivan sat at the head of the table, the expression on his face not exactly what Reid would consider cordial. While a bowl of watercress salad made its way around the table, Mariska said to Yana, "Reid's father is going to be our next senator."

Yana held up her wine glass. *"Gratulalok."*

"Thank you, but it might be a little early for congratulations." Reid scooped up a spoonful of dark, fragrant rice with vegetables. "We'll need to have an election first and make it official."

Yana met his gaze, her smile knowing. "One should always hold hope."

"I agree." Reid glanced at Tina, who quickly reached for her wineglass.

"So are you interested in politics yourself?" Yana asked.

He shook his head. "I'm just taking a month off from the family business to help establish a campaign headquarters."

"So, Reid," Mariska said, clearly wanting to steer the subject in a different direction, "I understand you come from a big family. Do you see yourself having children one day?"

He felt Rachel stiffen beside him, while Tina softly coughed. Ivan glared at his wife.

"I'm sure I will," Reid said evenly. "One day."

"When you find the right woman, of course." Mariska handed him a platter. "Chicken?"

Tina's cough turned to a choking sound, and Sophia slapped her on the back.

"Thanks." He speared a leg and set it on his plate. "This all looks and smells delicious. You must have been in the kitchen all day."

"It is nothing." Mariska waved a hand. "Rachel helped with most of the preparation. She is a wonderful cook, you know."

Rachel furrowed her brow. "I chopped the celery and onions, Mom."

"And so beautifully," Mariska said. "Every piece perfect."

Ivan's mouth pressed into a hard line as he stabbed a chicken breast.

"Tell Reid about your bingo win last night, Mariska," Yana said, sipping her wine. "It's such an interesting story."

Thrilled to repeat the story everyone else had already heard five times, Mariska leaned close to Reid. "I have only one number left, B7. Ivan, he has one, as well, B1."

In spite of being distracted by Tina's presence, Reid was truly trying to listen to Mariska. Until he felt a bare toe slide up his pant leg. He froze and looked at Tina, who appeared completely absorbed in her mother's story, then glanced at Sophia, who was casually sipping on a glass of ice water.

When the toe slid higher, Reid grabbed his own water glass to ward off the threatening cough, careful to keep his gaze on Mariska.

"The ball comes up, it is blue, so I know it is a B, and what number do they call?" Mariska slapped a hand to her chest. "B7!"

"It was a hundred dollars." Scowling, Ivan took his knife to his chicken. "You would think she won the lottery, the way she carries on."

"It is a hundred more than you won, Ivan Alexander." Mariska waved a fork at her husband.

The argument was without heat, but it was enough to distract Tina's parents for the moment. Reid looked at Tina, watched her gaze slowly lift to his. Though it was only for a split second, the look she flashed him was as hot as it was arousing.

He really needed to get this woman alone, he thought, taking a gulp of his wine. He hoped like hell it would be soon.

Mariska was serving strudel and coffee when the phone rang. When she started to rise, Rachel sprang out of her chair.

"I'll get it."

"If it is a salesman, hang up on him," Ivan yelled after Rachel, then looked at Reid. "A man cannot have a meal in peace with his family."

Not sure if the comment was directed at him, Reid simply nodded.

"Since when has this family had a peaceful meal?" Mariska said. "You are always grumbling about something."

Ivan frowned at his wife, then forked up a bite of strudel. "I do not grumble. I make observations."

Reid drew in a breath when Tina—he hoped it was Tina—ran her toes up his pant leg again. She was intentionally torturing him, he realized, and was already planning payback when Rachel returned.

"Salesman?" Ivan asked.

"Hang up." Rachel slid back into her seat.

A moment later, while Ivan and Mariska were still discussing how incredibly rude and inconsiderate some people were, Rachel cleared her throat, then looked at Reid and said, "Would you like to go to the movies?"

Phone call forgotten, Mariska beamed. "That is a wonderful idea."

Ivan scowled. "My daughter does not ask a man on a date."

"It's not a date," Rachel said quickly. "There's a new comedy at the cinema. Tina and Sophia said they wanted to see it, too. After we did the dishes, I thought we could all go."

He was beginning to get the picture, but Reid realized it had nothing to do with the movies. Obviously that phone call had been the source of Rachel's unexpected invitation. "I'd love to go."

"You and Reid go." Mariska was already rising from her seat. "Tina and Sophia will help me with the dishes."

"Katina and Sophia will go, too," Ivan decreed.

"Sorry." Sophia shook her head. "I'll help with the dishes, but I promised I'd help out in the office at the club tonight."

"Then Katina will go," Ivan said firmly. "It is settled."

Thank you, Ivan, Reid thought, and when he glanced at Tina, could see she was thinking the same.

It took a while to say their goodbyes, but once they were outside and away from the house, Rachel looked at Tina and Reid. "I'm sure you realize we aren't really going to the movies."

"I figured it out," he said with a nod.

When headlights flashed from a parked car down the street, Rachel hugged Tina, then hurried off.

Left alone in the darkness behind a tall hedge, Reid dragged Tina into his arms and kissed her. Placing her palms flat on his chest, she leaned into him and kissed him back.

"You taste like apples," he said against her lips.

"So do you."

He kissed her again, then whispered, "Well, that was interesting."

"Kissing me?" she teased. "Or having dinner with my parents?"

"Both."

"*Interesting* is not exactly the word I'd use." She blew out a breath. "More like horrific."

He grinned at her. "So you want to tell me exactly what you were doing back there at the dinner table?"

"What do you mean?"

"You know what I mean," he said, lifting a brow. "Sliding your toe up my leg. I nearly had a heart attack."

Furrowing her brow, she met his gaze. "I didn't touch your leg with my toe."

He felt a moment's panic, then saw the smile in her eyes and frowned at her.

"Very funny," he said, then pulled her close and slid his mouth to her neck. The hitch of her breath, her soft sigh, the slight trembling in her hands made his own pulse stutter.

"I asked you a question last night," he murmured, lifting his head. "I don't believe you ever truly answered me."

Her fingers moved restlessly over his chest. "What was that?"

"Will you come home with me?"

Her lashes slowly fluttered up. Smiling, she looked into his eyes. "I thought you'd never ask."

Eight

The penthouse was spacious. Marble foyer, high ceilings, rich, glossy hardwood floors. Antiques—an impressive, and expensive, mix of eighteenth- and nineteenth-century pieces—were artfully arranged throughout the large living room and parlor. Softly lit paintings, mostly oils, graced the hunter-green walls. From an art history class she'd taken at the local college, Tina knew that several of the paintings were nineteenth-century Southern artists.

More than a little intimidated, she stood in front of the wall-to-wall leaded windows overlooking Forsyth Park. A full moon shone silver on the thick treetops; downtown city lights twinkled in the dark. She could only imagine how spectacular the view from here would be during the day.

Wondering briefly if she would ever see that view,

she turned and strolled around the room, paused to admire a walnut Chippendale sideboard table, then moved on to examine the intricate leaf carvings on a mahogany framed mirror.

Engrossed in the detail of the frame, she didn't notice Reid come up behind her. He wrapped his arms around her before she could turn.

"Sorry. I had to return a call from Ian."

Her pulse jumped when she met his gaze in the mirror. "Everything all right?"

On the drive from her house, Reid had told Tina about the body being found in his family's attic and their suspicions that it might be his missing cousin, Victoria. Tina couldn't imagine what the entire Danforth family was going through right now, not knowing the truth and having to wait for days or even weeks before the results of the tests could be verified. Her heart went out to all of them, especially to Reid's aunt and uncle.

"Ian wanted to warn me that there's a hotshot reporter named Jasmine Carmody sniffing around." Reid's arms tightened around Tina. "Nicola wants to keep this situation quiet for as long as possible. Even the hint of a scandal so soon in the campaign could blow the election for my Dad."

"Can you really keep something like this from the press?"

"Not for long." He sighed. "Especially with an army of reporters skulking around every corner just waiting for the tiniest speck of dirt. But we might be able to hold off until we at least get some preliminary results from the DNA testing. That will help Nicola decide how to best handle the press.''

"I can't imagine living under a microscope like that,'' she said quietly. "I don't think I could stand it.''

"It's part of who I am.'' He shrugged. "Who my family is. I guess I just accept it.''

"I can certainly understand that.'' She smiled at him. "After spending the evening with my family, you probably wonder how I manage to get through a day without going crazy.''

He brought his face beside hers, grinned at her in the mirror. "I think your family is terrific, though I don't think your dad likes me too much. You know the saying 'if looks could kill'? It's amazing I made it out of your house alive tonight.''

She laughed softly at the absurdity, yet truth, of his statement. "My dad doesn't like any man who wants to date one of his daughters. He says that men just want one thing.''

"Smart man.'' Reid brushed his mouth along her neck, then moved up to nuzzle her ear.

The closeness of his body, his mouth just a few inches from her own, made it hard for Tina to think. She desperately wanted to turn in his arms, press her lips to his and ask him to take her to his bed, or just simply take her, but watching what he was doing to her in the mirror absolutely mesmerized her.

"I thought about you today,'' he whispered.

"Did you?'' Her breath quickened when his tongue flicked over her earlobe.

"Did you think about me?''

"No." Every nerve ending along her neck quivered.

He glanced at her in the mirror and smiled smugly. "Liar."

"Maybe a little," she admitted, heard the breathlessness in her own voice.

"Just a little?" He moved to her neck, rubbed his lips up and down the slender column of soft, sensitive flesh.

Her skin grew hot and tight, her bones soft. Afraid she might slide to the floor, she leaned back against his chest. "Maybe more than a little."

Keeping his eyes locked with hers, he smiled against her neck. "What did you think about?"

"Towels."

He lifted his head. "You thought about towels?"

"Actually, it was more about the expression on your face when my aunt walked in and that's all you were wearing."

"Me?" His smile widened. "You should have seen *your* face."

Just thinking about it now made her cheeks warm. "It's not every day a member of my family walks in and finds me with a naked man."

"I'm glad to hear that." He nipped at her neck. "Very glad."

His teeth on her skin sent shivers through her. His breath was hot on her throat. She felt her eyelids grow heavy, her blood thicken. Each and every beat of her heart echoed like a drum inside her brain.

"My aunt wants to photograph you," she managed to say, even as a whirlwind of heat spiraled through her mind and body.

He stilled, looked at her doubtfully. "Me?"

"In your towel." She watched him lift one brow. "But preferably without."

"Maybe some other time," he said, though his expression said more like "never." "I'm going to be a little busy for a while."

"Doing what?"

"This," Reid murmured, and turned his attention back to Tina's neck.

He couldn't get enough of the taste and feel of her. Watching her in the mirror aroused him like nothing he'd ever experienced before. The flutter of her thick lashes, the rise and fall of her breasts, the soft flush of desire on her cheeks. He slid his hands under her sweater, felt warm skin and soft cotton. She shivered when he cupped her breasts.

She fit perfectly. Firm, yet soft, and when he caressed her, he felt her nipples harden against his palms.

"Reid." She said his name on a ragged whisper, tried to turn in his arms.

"Don't move." He held her against him. "I want to look at you."

She stilled, held her breath when he reached for the hem of her sweater, then slowly pulled it over her head and tossed it aside.

Her bra was baby pink, simple cotton, and he didn't think he'd ever seen anything sexier in his life. Gently, he kneaded the firm, soft flesh, then slipped the fabric down and bared her breasts.

Her cheeks darkened with a blush, and she dropped her eyes.

"Look at me, Tina," he said hoarsely. "Keep your eyes on me."

He watched her lift her gaze to his, saw the fire in her eyes, the same fire that raced through his own blood and over his skin. He lowered his gaze and had to remind himself to breathe. She was so beautiful, her skin so soft and smooth. He brushed his thumbs over her rosy nipples, saw and felt them grow tighter under his touch.

Every inch of him wanted to take her now, right this second, standing right here. But he couldn't let go of this moment, not yet. He felt intoxicated by the sight and touch of her, wanted this feeling to last as long as he—as they both—could possibly stand it. Not a simple task when he wanted to touch her, kiss her everywhere at once.

So he concentrated on her breasts. Stroking, caressing, teasing. Pushing fabric away until there was only skin against skin, soft against rough, ivory against tan. He thought he might die if he didn't taste her soon, if he couldn't take her pearled nipple in his mouth, feel the hardness of her against his tongue.

On a moan her head fell back against his chest. And then her hands got busy.

She slid her hands up and down the outsides of his thighs, a slow, rhythmic movement...up, down, up again...gradually inching her way to the inside. When her fingertips skimmed the edge of his hardness, he sucked in a breath.

It shocked Tina that her knees were still able to hold her. Like warm wax, her body melted against Reid's, molding intimately so she felt every muscle of his chest against her back, the curve of her hips against his, the press of his erection against her buttocks. Watching what he was doing to her, with his hands on her breasts, his mouth on her throat and neck, was more than she could bear.

Didn't he know that? she thought, squirming against him. Didn't he know how much she wanted him, how desperately she needed him?

She took comfort in knowing that the sweet torture was not hers alone. His eyes had darkened with need, as well. His body had grown hard and tense, his breathing had turned ragged. If this was a contest as to who could last the longest without begging, she would surely—gladly—lose.

"Reid," she breathed his name, pressed herself firmly against him and moved back and forth, felt him grow harder still.

His hand moved down her stomach to the button on her slacks and popped it open. Tugging her zipper down, he slid his fingertips over her belly, then cupped her in his palm. When he pressed his lips to her ear and whispered what he wanted to do, she thought, *Yes, yes!* Please do that and more!

Moaning softly, she could only wonder when and how she'd become so shameless, so wanton. She felt as if she might burst into flames any moment, and when he began to stroke her, she did. A firestorm swept over her, and the fury of it consumed her.

"Look at me," she gasped.

His eyes, glinting dark with need, met hers.

"I need you," she whispered roughly. Taking hold

of his wrist, she moved her hips against him. "Inside me."

His jaw tightened, then he turned her toward him, dropping his mouth down on hers at the same time he lifted her up in his arms. She slid her arms around his neck and held on tight, the urgency overwhelming her ability to think of anything but satiating the raw, consuming need.

While walking with her to the bedroom, his mouth never left hers for more than a second. Kiss by kiss, touch by touch, their clothes fell away. Arms entwined, they tumbled onto the bed. She felt the mattress give beneath her, the downy cushion of a comforter, the slide of soft cotton on her back. The hard press of man.

Her breath caught, and she wrapped her arms around his shoulders as much to brace herself as to pull him closer. He bent his head to her neck, her shoulder, then to her breast. She arched upward on a moan when he took her into his mouth and suckled, arrows of white-hot pleasure shot from her breast to the V of her thighs. He used his tongue and teeth and lips on her; one moment he was gentle, the next he was rough. She couldn't decide which she liked better. Both thrilled her, aroused her to the edge of insanity.

When he finally moved between her legs and entered her, she slipped over that edge.

After what they'd shared the previous night, Tina wouldn't have thought it possible that this joining could be more. But somehow it was. This time she felt as if he took more than her body, more than her heart, but her very soul. In every way she was absolutely and completely vulnerable. She held back nothing, willingly gave all she was.

He thrust deeply inside the tight, hot glove of her body. Again and again. Long, slow strokes that gradually quickened. Like a drum beating faster, then faster still, pounding fiercely. They moved as one, the urgency now gripping them both.

She cried out when the first shudder rolled through her, dug her fingernails into the rippling muscles of his damp back. He took her hips in his hands, held her still as the second shudder shattered inside her.

She felt his climax stiffen his body. On a deep, harsh groan, he crushed her to him and shuddered.

Too spent to move, to speak, to even think, they sank into the mattress together. After minutes or hours, it was hard to say which, he rolled to his side and pulled her into his arms.

Laying her head and hand on his chest, she listened to, and felt, the heavy beat of his heart.

And she smiled.

When Reid woke, he had no sense of time. He glanced at the bedside table, then realized they'd only been asleep a few minutes. Tina stirred at the movement, then murmured a complaint when he slid out from under her.

"You're cold." He pulled down the bedclothes, then tucked her under the warmth of the covers.

Her eyes fluttered open as she rolled to her side and tucked her hands under her face. "I wasn't until you moved."

Light from the moon washed the walls in shades of

gray, sent shadows sliding across the floor. An over-whelming sense of peace and...wholeness? settled over the room.

Climbing under the covers beside Tina, he stretched out and leaned on an elbow, gazed down at her and grinned. "You look good in my bed, darling."

Her eyes met his as she slid a fingertip from his shoulder to his hand. "You have such a big one."

His grin widened. "Thanks."

Rolling her eyes, she slid her fingertip to his chest and pushed. "Bed."

"Oh." He feigned a hurt look.

"Very masculine."

His heart lurched when her fingertip slid down his chest to his rib cage. "I'm glad you like it."

It wasn't so much what she was doing to him as it was what she *wasn't* doing. With her finger tracing the outline of his bottom rib, she seemed quite content to touch him, but stay within the parameters of "safe" territory.

Not that her touching him anywhere was exactly what he'd call safe, Reid thought.

When she ever so slightly inched her way down-ward, he sucked in a breath and covered her hand with his. "Tina, look at me."

She lifted her gaze to his, and he realized she didn't have to touch him at all to turn him on. All she had to do was look at him with those languid bed-room eyes.

"I'm not going to pretend I'm interested in Rachel anymore."

Her hand stilled, then she rolled to her back. "I

know," she said, closing her eyes. "I don't want you to."

Leaning over her, he brushed his mouth against hers. "We can talk to your parents tomorrow and—"

"No!" Her eyes snapped open. "I'll need to talk to Rachel first, to prepare her. Then I'll talk to my parents."

"I understand that family dynamics can be complicated. Lord knows mine gives new meaning to the word. But you're twenty-four years old."

She shook her head. "You don't understand my father. When it comes to Sophia and Rachel and me, he's more than unreasonable—he's irrational and inflexible."

"What could he object to?" Reid asked, then cocked his head and grimaced. "Well, other than the fact I've seduced his youngest daughter and taken her virginity. So how big are the knives in his kitchen, anyway?"

"Just be glad he's a baker, not a butcher." Smiling, she pressed a kiss to his jaw, then dropped her gaze. "Reid, I want you to know that just because you... because we, ah, slept together, I'm not expecting, I mean, I'm not asking for any kind of—" She blew out a breath. "You know."

"Commitment?" The word felt odd on his tongue. He had to roll it around in his mouth, found the taste wasn't as bitter as he'd thought it would be.

If anything, he suddenly realized with startling clarity, the taste was just right.

Yet here Tina was, Reid thought irritably, intently trying to explain to him that she wasn't expecting, or asking, for a relationship. He frowned at her. "Are you dumping me, Tina?"

"No, of course not." Her gaze snapped back up. "I just think you, *we,* should be open and honest with each other."

"Haven't we been?"

"I just don't want any misunderstanding between us."

"Looks to me like there already is, sweetheart." She gasped when he took her by the shoulders and rolled to his back, bringing her on top of him. "Look, I don't know exactly what's going on here between us, but I do know I want to be with you, openly and publicly."

"I'd like to be with you, too," she said softly, then pressed her smile to his mouth. "But your family, your father's campaign—"

"My father's campaign has nothing to do with you and me, Tina. Who I see personally and what I do in my private life is my business."

"And every newspaper and magazine reporter's in Savannah," she added.

"That's always a possibility," he said with a nod. "I'm a Danforth. I can't stop being who I am."

Her eyes softened as she touched his cheek. "I wouldn't want you to, Reid."

Her hand on his cheek, such a simple, gentle gesture, made his chest hitch. He couldn't remember any woman who'd ever made him feel this way. No woman who had ever mattered so much.

He took her lovely, delicate face in his hands and

brought her mouth to his, wondered if he would ever get enough of the sweet taste of her.

He certainly intended to try.

Tracing the seam of her lips with his tongue, he slid inside the honeyed softness. Her tongue met his, mating, stroking, slowly growing more urgent. He felt more than heard the moan from deep in her throat, and the slight forward thrust of her hips heated his blood.

Wanting, needing more, he deepened the kiss, slanted his mouth against hers over and over. He ran his hands down her back, cupped the round softness of her firm bottom, arched his hips up to press intimately into the V of her legs.

They were both breathing heavily when she rose upward, then slowly came back down onto the hard length of him, inch by torturous inch. He pressed himself deeply inside her, his hands tightly gripping her hips.

And then she began to move. Slowly at first, drawing out the intense pleasure until it became unbearable. With every thrust of her hips, the rhythm built, spiraled. The fever swept through them like a storm, wild and fierce. Powerful.

Eyes closed, hair tumbling around her shoulders, she tossed her head back on a sharp cry as her climax shuddered through her. He crushed his hips to hers, driving himself into her again and again, until his body convulsed with the same release.

She collapsed on him, gasping for breath, murmuring something incoherent. Struggling to breathe, himself, he wrapped his arms around her, brushed his mouth over her temple and kissed her cheek.

While their hearts and breathing slowed and their minds cleared, he held her close, smiled when she sighed and snuggled against his chest. "No more sneaking around," he reminded her.

"Tomorrow," she murmured on a nod. "I'll talk to my parents tomorrow."

Nine

Tina came into the bakery through the back entrance, winced at the bright tinkling of the bell that signaled the opening of the door. On a daily basis, she never even noticed the sound. But today, considering the fact she was an hour late, that little brass bell seemed to blare with the fervor of a bastille trumpeter.

Once, Tina remembered, when Sophia was sixteen, she'd managed to wrench the clangor out of the bell so she could meet a boyfriend in the back garden. But their father had caught on quickly enough. The boyfriend had been banished, Sophia grounded, and the bell replaced with a stronger, louder, daughter-proof model. While Mariska held charge at the front door, from the kitchen, Ivan kept track of the comings and goings through the back door. No one sneaked in, no one sneaked out. As teenagers, it had driven the Alexander girls crazy, but as adults, Tina had never given it much thought.

Until today.

Today, she thought with a smile, she'd overslept in the arms of the man she loved.

A shiver ran through her that had nothing to do with the cool air coming in through the still-open back door. When she'd wakened this morning in Reid's penthouse, with his broad chest pressed against her back and his muscled arm draped possessively around her waist, she'd had to pinch herself. *Enjoy the moment,* she'd told herself. Don't think about the future. Don't let yourself hope, or wish, for too much. Be happy with what you have now.

But what if, she thought. What if maybe, just maybe…

A breeze whispered over her neck, and an unreasonable dread shivered through her. She closed the door, wincing again at the bell's clanging, then glanced at her watch. Rachel would be in her office already, and even though Tina knew they needed to talk, she didn't dare take the time now.

Hurrying down the hallway, she stuck her head around the corner and cringed at the sight of the long customer line. Her mother was working the register while her aunt helped fill orders. Billy, the counter clerk Tina had just hired, was working the coffee counter.

She wondered briefly where Jason was, then realized he was probably already preparing to go to Los Angeles with his band.

Terrific. One more straw on the camel's back.

At least Yana had come in to help this morning, Tina thought. That would save the day from being a complete calamity. Tina caught her aunt's attention and gave her an is-it-safe-to-enter look. Yana nodded, then pressed a finger to her lips.

Sucking in a breath to calm her nerves, Tina walked behind the counter and grabbed an apron.

"Katina." Her mother frowned at her. "Where have you been?"

"I'm sorry, I—" She glanced at her aunt, who shook her head.

"Never mind." Mariska cut Tina off with a swipe of her hand. "We will talk about this later. Take the register while I package Mrs. Green's brioche."

A crash from the kitchen, then mumbled cursing, had Mariska shaking her head. "There will be no living with that man today."

"I'll go talk to him," Yana said, then winked at Tina. "He'll be fine."

Tina swallowed the lump of tension in her throat, grateful for the temporary reprieve. Even though this was not looking like the best of days to have a father/daughter talk, she'd made a promise to Reid, and for both their sakes, she was determined to keep that promise.

It was another fifteen minutes before the morning rush finally thinned out, and with only two customers in the bakery, both of them sitting at tables, and her mother and Yana in the kitchen, Tina knew she had to "seize the moment," as the saying went. It was time for her, and for Rachel, to tell their parents the truth. It was time for them to realize that their daughters were not children anymore, but adults.

"Billy, watch the counter," she said to the new clerk. "I'll be back in a minute."

She was already heading for Rachel's office when the bakery door opened and Reid walked in.

No! she wanted to say. *You can't be here yet.* She was torn between throwing her arms around him or throwing him out.

When he walked straight toward her, her heart stopped.

For a moment she almost thought he was going to kiss her, but he didn't, just looked at her and smiled.

Her insides turned soft and warm.

Quickly she looked at the customers to see if they'd noticed who had walked in. When it appeared they hadn't, she grabbed his hand and pulled him into the hallway out of sight.

"Reid—"

His mouth caught hers, and for a moment she leaned against him, her pulse quickening as she returned the kiss. Oh, he smelled so good, a woodsy aftershave, and he tasted like mint. She wanted to kiss him all over.

Somehow she managed to come to her senses and stepped back.

"You shouldn't be here now," she said, still breathless from his kiss.

"I know." Sighing, he shoved his hands into his pockets. "I couldn't help myself."

In spite of her nerves, she smiled, then folded her arms and took another step back before she did something she'd regret, like wrap herself around him and kiss him again.

"This isn't a good time." Keeping her voice low, she glanced over her shoulder toward the kitchen. "I'm not sure what's going on, but my father's on the warpath this morning."

"Have you told him about us?"

She shook her head. "I got to work so late I didn't have a chance, and he's been in such a mood, I think it's better to wait."

"Why don't you and I go now?" he said quietly. "Together."

"It's not that simple." She closed her eyes and hugged her arms tightly around her. "You don't know what it's like when—"

"Katina."

At the sound of her father's voice in the hallway behind her, Tina's heart dropped. Slowly, very slowly, she turned and faced him. The look of fury on his face turned her blood to ice.

Ivan's gaze snapped to Reid. "You. In my kitchen."

"Yes, sir."

Tina touched his arm as he moved past her. "Reid," she whispered. "You don't have—"

"It's all right," he said with a nod. "It's time."

Heart racing, she followed Reid and her father into the kitchen, where her mother and Yana were dusting powdered sugar on cooled nut cookies. "Dad—"

"Quiet." Her father pointed a finger at her. "This is not your concern, Katina."

Not my concern? Too stunned to even respond, she simply stared at her father.

"Were you with my daughter last night?" Ivan demanded.

"Yes, sir."

"Ivan, keep hold of your temper." Wiping her hands, Mariska stepped closer to her husband. "We should discuss this calmly."

"Calmly!" He broke into a string of Hungarian phrases that Tina had never heard before and couldn't make out. "You think I should be calm when our daughter spends the night out with this man?"

"With all respect, sir," Reid said without raising his voice or batting an eye. "I'd like to say—"

"Please." Tina looked at Reid. "Let me explain."

"How can you explain for your sister?" Ivan narrowed his eyes as he looked at Tina. "When she gets here, she will speak for herself."

When she gets here? It took a beat to sink in. They were talking about *Rachel,* Tina realized. And what did they mean "when she gets here?"

"Rachel's not here yet?" Tina asked carefully.

Mariska bottom lip quivered. "She did not come home last night, or to work this morning. She did not even call."

Tina looked from her father, who had his beefy arms folded over his wide chest, then to her aunt, who shook her head.

"This is unbelievable." Tina looked up at the ceiling and sighed, then squared her shoulders. "Mom... Dad, Rachel's fine, but she didn't spend the night with Reid."

"The man just admitted it," Ivan shouted, then glared at Reid. "I demand to know where my daughter is."

"She's right here. With me."

All heads turned at the sound of Jason's voice. He stood at the back kitchen entrance, his arm locked securely around Rachel's waist.

"She was with me last night," Jason said, meeting Ivan's eye.

Uh-oh. Tina heard her mother gasp, then watched her father's face turn deep red and his eyes bulge. Here it comes.

"We got married." Beaming with happiness, Rachel held up her left hand to display the gold band on her third finger. "I'm Mrs. Jason Burns."

Rachel's announcement seemed to suck the air out of the room. No one spoke, no one moved.

"I love your daughter." Jason looked at Rachel and smiled. "And she loves me. I want to spend my life with her."

"Please be happy for us," Rachel said, her eyes filling with tears. "Please. I love him so much."

Breath held, Tina waited for her parents to say something, *anything,* but the shock hadn't worn off yet. They were still frozen in place, their eyes wide.

Maybe this wasn't going to be such a good time to tell her parents about Reid, after all, Tina thought.

It was Yana who moved first. Wiping her hands on a towel, she moved across the kitchen and wrapped her arms around both Rachel and Jason. "May you be blessed with happiness, health and many children."

"Well, that's the rest of the good news." Rachel

hugged her aunt back, then looked at her parents tim-
idly. "We're going to have a baby."

Gasping once again, Mariska clutched a fist to her
chest. Ivan went from red to purple.

A baby? Rachel was having a baby?

Her parents forgotten for the moment, Tina rushed
to her sister and new brother-in-law and threw her
arms around them. "When...how..."

"I wasn't sure until yesterday." Rachel wiped at
her tears. "That's why I didn't get a chance to tell
you, and then last night, when you went with Reid and
I—" Rachel bit her lip when she realized what she'd
said.

"Stop!" Ivan's bellow rattled the pans. "Everyone
stop right now."

They all froze.

His fists on his hips, Ivan stomped across the
kitchen and narrowed his eyes at Rachel. "You got
married to Jason and are having a baby."

Rachel nodded hesitantly.

Ivan swung a look at Tina. "And *you* were with
this man—" he glared at Reid "—last night."

Tina swallowed the lump in her throat and nodded.

A muscle twitched in Ivan's jaw. He turned slowly
and looked at his wife. "How could this happen?"

"What's happened?"

It was Sophia who spoke. She stood in the kitchen
doorway, took in the look on everyone's faces, plus
the way Rachel and Jason were wrapped around each
other, then arched a brow and said, "Oh."

Calmly, so calmly it frightened everyone, Ivan removed his apron and walked out of the room.

No one moved or spoke for a full ten seconds, then Yana let out a breath and said, "Well. I'd say that went well."

"My baby." Eyes overflowing with tears, Mariska opened her arms and rushed to Rachel. "I am going to be a grandmother."

And then Mariska was hugging everyone, including Reid, though she did grab his arms and frown at him for a moment before she sighed heavily, then hugged him again.

"Reid." Tina touched his arm. "I'm going to go talk to my father."

"I'll go with you."

"It's better if I go alone right now," she said, shaking her head. "Please."

He sighed, then nodded. "I'll be next door."

She found her father in the garden, standing by the small pond, staring down at the rippling water. The morning air was beginning to warm as the sun rose higher, and somewhere overhead in the branches of a magnolia tree, a songbird called to its mate.

He didn't turn when she approached, and she wasn't certain if he hadn't heard her, or if he was avoiding her. She stood quietly, several feet away and watched him, realized how long it had been since she'd truly looked at her father. He had always been a big man, strong, with shoulders broad enough to carry the world, she'd thought growing up.

Looking at him now, with those shoulders slightly bent and a distinguished touch of gray at his temples, her heart swelled with love. She couldn't bear it if he turned away from her, or from Rachel.

She stepped closer, was about to speak when he said, "Do you remember when we built this pond, Katina?"

His question stopped her. "I was ten," she said after a moment. "We lived upstairs, over the bakery."

"I mixed the cement, you and your sisters placed every rock exactly where they are now."

Nodding, she moved beside him. "You took us to the riverfront fair and let us each win a fish at the ping-pong toss."

"You named yours Gilbert." He turned then. "But you called it Gil."

She stared at him in wonder. "That was fourteen years ago. How could you remember that?"

"You are my baby," he said evenly. "You, your sisters. All of you. How can I forget?"

Tears welled in her eyes as she met his gaze. When he opened his arms, she moved into the comfort there. She couldn't remember how long it had been since he'd held her like this. Since she'd wanted him to.

"How can you, and Rachel and Sophia, how can you do this to me?" he said, his voice edged with anger. "To your mother."

Her heart sank. She'd wanted so desperately for him to understand and to accept she wasn't a child anymore. Lifting her head, she looked up at him, searching for the words.

"How can you grow up?" he said more softly, then touched her cheek and shook his head. "It is not right."

Relief poured through her. "I love you."

"And do you love him?" he asked.

She hesitated, then slowly nodded.

Her father sighed. "Does he love you?"

"I know he cares for me," she said. "But his family, our lives, are so different. I don't know if there's a place for me there."

"Ah. I see. This can be a problem." It was a long moment before her father spoke, as if he were carefully considering what Tina had said. "When your mother married me, your grandfather never spoke to her again."

Confused, Tina looked up at her father. "But I thought he died when Mom when a teenager."

"Your mother was eighteen, I was nineteen when I asked for her hand." Ivan's mouth pressed into a hard line. "A common man marrying a woman whose great-grandmother was a countess. He thought I was arrogant."

Tina had never heard there was a countess in her lineage, but as intriguing as it was, she realized this wasn't the time to ask. "You *are* arrogant."

"And you are impudent," he said, frowning. "But that was not the only reason he would not speak to your mother."

"Then what was?"

Ivan met his daughter's gaze, then sighed heavily. "Come sit, Katina," he said softly. "It is time I tell you the truth."

Reid paced the length of the back office in the campaign headquarters, wondering what was taking Tina so long. There hadn't been any explosions next door yet, nor had Ivan charged through the door breathing fire, so at least that much was a positive.

He wasn't used to waiting and it was driving him crazy. In fact, the operative word here was *crazy*. Everything about this entire situation was insane. A smarter, wiser man would have stayed away, he thought, would walk—no *run*—away. There were bound to be endless complications, and who the hell needed complications?

"Not me," he said to himself, then turned to pace the length of the office again. "I like things simple and easy," he told himself, and glanced at his wristwatch.

So what the hell was taking her so long?

He supposed she had her hands full at the moment. With her father finding out she'd spent the night with a man, then Rachel getting married *and* being pregnant, Reid imagined the dust was still flying.

What he found odd was that he hadn't wanted to leave, that he'd wanted to stay and be a part of all that dust. And that was *really* crazy.

Turning to pace again, he shoved his hands into his pockets. Dammit, where was she?

He started for the door, then stopped himself. He couldn't go back over there. Not yet. He'd give her another half hour, maybe even forty-five minutes. It wasn't as if he didn't have anything to do. He had five messages to return, one from Ian warning him that Jasmine Carmody had been snooping around at one of D&D's coffeehouses, the rest were from his shipping office regarding a lost container coming in from the Maximilian Paper account overseas. He knew he should handle that problem first, before he went back to the bakery.

He reached for the phone, punched in his office number, then slammed the phone back down.

Dammit!

He was heading for the door when he heard the light knock. Annoyed, he threw it open. "What!"

Startled, Tina took a step back. "I...I'm sorry. I can come back late—"

Grabbing her arm, he dragged her inside his office, kicking the door closed as he pulled her into his arms.

She stiffened when he caught her mouth with his, then relaxed and slid her arms around his neck. Her lips parted and he flicked his tongue over hers, a rough, deep, demanding kiss. Possessive. He could have tasted her forever like this, held her forever, but he finally, reluctantly, lifted his head and gazed down at her. "I had to do that first."

Her lips were still damp and rosy from his kiss, so tempting. He bent his head again.

"No." She placed a hand on his chest and he could feel her fingers trembling.

"You okay?"

"I...I don't know what I am."

Her voice was so distant, so strange, it worried him.

When she stepped out of his arms and turned away, he clenched his jaw. "Look, I know this is hard on your parents and it's a lot for one day, but dammit, we aren't kids. Just because they don't want you to see me—"

"No." She turned back, leveled her gaze with his. "That's not it at all."

What he saw in her eyes, the bleak emptiness, made his gut twist. "Then what?"

She sighed heavily, then folded her arms close. "When my father was a teenager, he was an apprentice in his country. He worked at the Castle Marcel under a man named Wilheim, who was the head baker."

"Why are you—"

"Please." She put up a hand. "Just listen."

Though he thought he might explode, Reid pressed his lips tightly together.

"There was no king or queen at the castle," Tina said. "Just a duke. But that's not relevant. Wilheim is."

When she paused, it took Reid every ounce of willpower he had not to rush her, but clearly she was struggling to gather her thoughts.

"According to my father," she finally went on, "Wilheim hated him, humiliated him every chance he got, publicly and privately. After four years, when my father turned nineteen, he'd decided he'd had enough and left. Wilheim lied and told the constable that my father had stolen Castle Marcel's secret recipes, recipes that had been passed down for generations. There was a warrant issued for my father's arrest."

In the corporate world, Reid knew that recipes of any food business were highly guarded, kept under lock and key and sophisticated alarm systems. And though it was a white-collar crime, it was still a crime.

"Isn't it a little extreme for Wilheim to have your father arrested?" Reid asked.

"Wilheim hated my father," Tina said. "Even

though all the recipes my father took were his own, they were recipes that Wilheim had taken credit for. Wilheim was worried he would be found out.''

''Surely your father could have proven himself innocent,'' Reid argued. ''The courts would have exonerated him.''

''Maybe, maybe not.'' She sighed. ''Wilheim had connections in high places. My father was young and afraid he would rot in prison. So he and my mother left the country on a merchant ship and were married. He worked in the galley to support them. When they came to America, they changed their name, moved from New York to Florida, then ended up in Savannah just before Sophia was born.''

She looked so pale, Reid thought. Her eyes so empty. And for the first time, he felt the fear snake through him.

''Tina. Sit.'' She stiffened when he took her arm, but he held on and tugged her to a chair, then knelt beside her. ''That was thirty years ago. Wilheim is probably dead by now.''

She shook her head. ''He's not dead.''

''So, what difference does it make?'' Reid said. ''He couldn't possibly still be angry.''

''Oh, but he is,'' she said quietly. ''When my father left, he did take something of Wilheim's.''

''What was that?''

''My mother. Wilheim is my grandfather.''

Whoa. Reid whistled through his teeth, then sat in the chair beside Tina. ''Oh,'' was all he could manage to say.

''Yeah. Oh.''

They were both silent for a moment, then Tina said, "My mother has called my grandfather several times over the years and tried to mend the rift, but he refuses. He insists he can still have my father arrested. My mother has never told him their new name or where we live, in case he tries to cause trouble."

"It will never stick, not after all this time. A good lawyer will clear him."

"My father is worried that even an accusation of being a thief will bring shame to his family. It's one of the reasons he's always been so protective of us, worrying that someday he might be found out."

"But your mother was happy when she thought I was interested in Rachel," Reid insisted.

"She was too excited at the prospect of one of her daughters marrying a Danforth to think about repercussions to the family," Tina said. "My father is innocent but innocent people are ruined everyday, Reid. I don't have to tell you that."

What she was saying was true, Reid knew. No matter how innocent a person truly was, accusations hung around like a bad smell. "Look, Tina, I know how difficult this might seem to you, but we—"

"It's not difficult, it's impossible. And I'm only telling you all this so you'll understand." She stood, looked down at him. "I can't jeopardize my family, and I won't jeopardize yours, either. If we continued to see each other, the media would be just as interested in my family as they are yours, and they'd be looking for dirt. Everyone would be hurt."

"Dammit, Tina." He rose and took hold of her arm. "We'll find a way to—"

"There is no 'we,' Reid," she said quietly, pulling her arm back. "There can't be. Not now. Not ever."

He wanted to shake her. Wanted to argue, to yell, throw something, even. But the cold conviction in her eyes told him that nothing was going to get through to her.

So he said nothing. Just felt his gut tighten and his stomach clench as he watched her turn, open the door and walk out of his life.

Ten

"It will not be too big, I have decided. No more than two hundred. Tina and Sophia, you will help me with the menu. Yana, you will take the pictures, of course."

Even though ten days had passed since Rachel and Jason had gotten married and left for Los Angeles, Mariska had not stopped talking about the impending reception. No one bothered to mention to her that she'd repeated herself at least a hundred times. She was too caught up in the excitement of her daughter's marriage to listen to anyone but herself. And the baby, good heavens! Mariska Alexander was going to be a grandmother, and she made sure that everyone knew.

While her mother rattled on and her father cleaned his oven, Tina dried the cake pans that Sophia and Yana had washed. It was the end of a long, busy day at the bakery, and rather than go home, Tina had stayed to help clean. If she kept busy, she didn't think as much.

It hurt to think. For that matter, it hurt to breathe.

"And the cake! Ivan, you must create something special, so special that people will cry at the mere sight of it, let alone the taste."

Just the mention of Rachel's wedding cake *did* make Tina feel like crying. She was happy for her sister, of course, and for Jason, but with her own heart shattered into tiny pieces, it was more than a little difficult to get excited about a wedding reception.

Reid had made several attempts to talk with her since she'd walked out of his office, but she'd coolly and quickly ended any discussion he'd tried to have with her. What was the point in discussing what could never be? It was impossible to date openly, and dangerous to date secretly.

Maybe it was for the best, she thought. They hadn't known each other that long. Surely it would only hurt more later when he decided to move on, she told herself. But it didn't make her feel any better, and she couldn't imagine any pain worse than what she felt in her chest right now.

"Abraham Danforth's secretary called this morning and ordered three hundred pastries for Saturday," Mariska said to everyone. "We will need extra hands to have them ready for delivery by four."

Tina's fingers tightened on the towel in her hand. Just hearing the name Danforth made her heart skip, but she forced herself to remain calm. She knew her family was concerned about her since she'd ended her relationship with Reid. She didn't want them to worry or fuss over her, was afraid she might break down if they did.

She'd convinced them all she'd be fine, that Reid had understood why they could never be more than friends. It was ridiculous, of course. She knew she could never truly just be friends with Reid. Not when every time she saw him she wanted to wrap herself around him, wanted to feel his heartbeat against hers, his mouth on her lips.

She shook the dangerous thoughts off, set down the pan she'd dried, then picked up another without missing a beat.

"We will all have to be ready for the party by six-thirty," Mariska continued. "Cocktails are at seven and dinner is at eight."

Party? Tina's hand stilled on the cake pan.

The party. At Crofthaven. What seemed like a life-time ago, Nicola had invited all the volunteers at the orientation meeting to come to a campaign-kick-off celebration. Tina silently groaned. She'd completely forgotten. And when she realized the party was only two days from now, her heart jackhammered against her ribs.

Oh, dear God! She couldn't possibly go. Couldn't look at Reid, couldn't even be in the same room with him. Here at the bakery was one thing, but at a party? Without the formality of work and the solid wall of a counter between them, she would fall apart for certain.

"Tina?"

She glanced up sharply and looked at her mother. "What?"

"Will you be all right?" Mariska asked softly. "You do not have to go if you do not want to."

"Of course I'm going." The way everyone was watching her, with sympathy in their eyes, she knew she *had* to go. She needed to prove to her family that she was over Reid. This would be the perfect opportunity. She would laugh, she would smile, maybe even flirt a little, though she'd rather pick blackberries in high heels, naked.

She imagined the feeling would be somewhat the same.

"Are you sure?" Sophia asked softly.

"I told you." Tina shrugged casually and reached for another pan to dry. "Reid and I are still friends. I'll be fine."

Her father grunted, and she wasn't sure if the sound was directed at her or the oven he was cleaning.

It didn't matter, she told herself. As difficult as it would be, she would go to the party, and for everyone's sake, she would pretend she was having a wonderful time.

It was nearly midnight when Reid walked through his front door. He'd spent the day at his father's campaign headquarters, but the escalating crisis with the lost container had kept him at his Danforth & Co. office until after eleven. Maximilian Paper Products' shipping department had been screaming at Reid's office to find the container immediately, and Reid had decided to handle the problem himself. Fortunately, the error had turned up on Maximilian's end when Reid discovered that one of the office workers had

transposed a docking number. Once the mistake had
been cleared, Reid had finally been able to go home.

Not that it much mattered to him where he went. If
anything, he'd rather stay at work and deal with angry
clients. It was much easier than coming home to an
empty apartment. Much easier than sleeping alone in
his bed, thinking about Tina. Remembering the way
she'd looked lying in his bed, with her hair tousled
and her eyes glazed with passion.

He missed her smile, the way her brow arched when
she was surprised. The way she said his name. When
she was annoyed, it was ''Reid!'' short and clipped.
When she smiled, it was ''Reid,'' warm and soft.
When they'd made love it was breathless, ''Reid...''

He couldn't get her out of his head, though God
knew he'd tried. Other than a polite hello every time
he'd gone into the bakery, she hadn't actually spoken
to him for ten days. Ten days, dammit!

He dropped his keys on his entry table and dragged
a hand through his hair. If she refused to talk to him,
how the hell were they supposed to work out this problem?

But the real question was, could they?

Sighing, he slipped out of his coat, tossed it over a
living room chair, then sank down on the sofa. He'd
gone over what she'd told him a hundred times, looking for a loophole somewhere, but he hadn't found
one. Any kind of open confrontation with her grandfather would put her family in peril, and if he and Tina
continued to see each other, the press would most certainly find out and dig into her family's background.
Ultimately they would find out something. They al-

ways did. And no matter how small something was, how insignificant, it would be sensationalized. His father's campaign would be hurt, and though Reid seriously doubted Tina's father would be deported or go to jail, he still stood the danger of his reputation being tarnished.

The media and the gossipmongers would have a field day.

Unbuttoning his shirt, he closed his eyes on a weary sigh and laid his head back. He could almost smell her sweetness, could almost taste it, could almost hear her laugh, her sigh. Everything about her lingered here.

On an oath, he rose and walked to his liquor cabinet, pulled out a bottle of Glenlivet, then put it back. Too smooth, he thought, and grabbed a bottle of cheap whiskey instead. He needed something with more of a bite, something he could sink his teeth into.

Pouring a healthy shot, he tossed it back, felt it burn all the way down, then poured another, hoping like hell it would wash away the lump in his chest that refused to go away.

Crofthaven received its guests with uniformed valets and thousands of twinkling white lights on the front lawn trees. Once whisked inside and coats checked, they were greeted by a five-piece band playing soft pop music and white-gloved waiters serving shrimp toast, salmon-mousse-stuffed cherry tomatoes, melted brie in puff pastry and spicy meatballs in wine sauce. Drinks were available from a full-service bar, while roving wine and soda attendants offered refills for the thirsty crowd.

By Crofthaven standards, 150 people was not a large party. Abraham and Nicola had invited only the first group of volunteers from the main campaign headquarters and a dozen or so of the campaign's largest donors. The press, a carefully selected few, had also been treated to the evening's festivities. They swarmed through the crowded ballroom like hornets, buzzing with questions disguised as casual conversation, hoping, praying, for the tiniest piece of breaking news, good or bad, though any reporter worth his or her salt knew that bad always made bigger, more interesting headlines.

Standing by the closed patio French doors with Ian, Reid took in all the people, their smiling faces, bright eyes and animated conversations. Though he'd never much cared for parties, he'd never especially detested them, either. Until tonight.

Tonight his neck hurt from sleeping on his sofa for the past week; his vision was blurred from sitting at his computer all day while he'd entered docking manifests into a log; and to top it off, he had an annoying twitch in the corner of his left eye.

When Albert Johnson, one of his father's wealthiest contributors and staunch supporters walked by, Reid forced a smile and thought his face might break.

"Hard to believe that only a week ago police lines and the coroner's office were center stage here," Ian said quietly to Reid. "It almost seems as if we dreamed the whole thing."

Nodding, Reid snagged a glass of red wine from a

passing tray. He felt that way about Tina, too. As if being with her had never truly happened. That he'd had the ultimate dream that had turned into a nightmare.

Getting drunk the other night hadn't helped, he thought, taking a gulp of his wine, but what the hell, maybe he'd try it again. "What's really hard to believe is that it hasn't leaked to the press yet."

"Nicola has a statement ready to go. Two, actually, one if we discover it is Vickie, and the other if it isn't. In the meantime," Ian said somberly, "we wait."

Reid glanced at his aunt and uncle, who were on the other side of the ballroom. Though they were both smiling and shaking hands with people, Reid knew that on the inside they were anxious and more than a little afraid of what the coroner's results would show.

He also knew they would have preferred not to show up tonight but had worried that their absence might have led to questions, questions that always led to suspicions that there were problems in the Danforth family. Problems that the other candidates would love to pounce on and blow out of proportion.

Which is the exact same reason I'm here tonight, Reid thought. He sure didn't feel like shaking hands and making idle conversation, either. What he felt like was putting on a pair of boxing gloves and punching off some of the rage that had been building in him since Tina had walked out of his life.

He was going absolutely crazy.

He'd hoped that as each day passed and he stayed away from her he wouldn't miss her so much, that he wouldn't think about her every minute of the day and dream about her at night. What had happened was he missed her more. Not even burying himself in his work and the campaign had eased the tension burning his blood.

And though he'd told himself he didn't want to be here tonight and he'd only come for appearance's sake, he knew the real reason he was here. The only reason he was here.

He'd hoped that Tina would come.

When Ivan and Mariska had walked in several minutes ago without their youngest daughter, Reid's hope had disintegrated. He supposed he understood why she hadn't come, but dammit, if he couldn't do anything else, he'd at least wanted to *talk* to her. To *see* her. At this point he was willing to take whatever crumb he could find.

While he continued to scan the ballroom, just in case he'd missed her come in, he sipped the glass of wine and did his best to listen to Ian discuss a new coffee he'd added to the already extensive menu at D&D's.

"...full body and the taste is a little sweet..."

Tina has a sweet taste, Reid thought. And her body...hell, that body drove him mad.

"...and a smoothness about it that should make it..."

Smooth. Tina's skin was silky smooth, like rose petals.

"...blended is selling well, though there seems to be a preference to hot..."

Definitely a preference to hot. The image of Tina

lying naked under him, whispering his name, her body moving in rhythm with his—*dammit!*

He missed everything about her.

"Something wrong with your eye?" Ian asked, interrupting Reid's wayward thoughts.

"No." Scowling, Reid touched the corner of his left eye.

Ian leaned closer. "It's twitching."

"It's nothing."

"Nothing." Ian chuckled. "Right. Unless nothing is about Tina."

"Let it rest, Ian."

"Sure you don't want to talk about it?" Ian grinned. "Since you're looking like a lovestruck pup, might as well get it off your chest."

"Are you intentionally trying to provoke me?" Reid asked tightly. "Or does it just come naturally?"

"Neither." Ian's grin widened. "I just want to watch the look on your face when I tell you that Tina just walked in with her aunt."

Reid's head snapped around at Ian's comment. He thought for a moment that Ian was messing with his mind. But then he saw her, standing at the ballroom entrance, and his heart stopped, along with his ability to think or breathe.

She wore red. Not siren red, but deep, deep red, more the color of a fine claret. The dress shimmered snugly around her slim shape, scooped low over her breasts, but stopped demurely at her knees. Her heels were high and shiny black, open at the toes and wrapped around her narrow ankles. She'd done something different to her hair, sort of swept half up and let the other half tumble around her soft shoulders. Her lips were red, too, but her eyes were smoky.

When she turned and he saw the back of her dress— a lace-up, corset look that exposed just enough skin to make a man need to see more—his heart jumped up into his throat.

"Can I have her?" Ian sounded hopeful. "'Cause if you're not going to—"

"Shut up, Ian," Reid growled. "Don't say it, don't even think it, unless you want us to be headline news on the *Savannah Morning* tomorrow."

Laughing, Ian rocked back on his heels. "Whatever you say, bro."

Keeping his gaze on Tina, Reid shoved his glass of wine into Ian's hand and made his way through the crowd.

"Tina, for heaven's sake—" Yana slipped an arm through her niece's "—if you don't breathe, you're going to pass out."

"I *am* going to pass out." Tina clung to her aunt's arm, turned them both and made an attempt to drag Yana back to the door they'd just come through. "Please, I can't do this. I know I told you and every-one else I was over Reid, but I lied."

"I know, Katina." Yana patted Tina's arm and turned them back around again. "We all know. We lied when we told you we believed you."

"You did? They did?" So much for her acting abil-ities.

"Of course, dear."

"Then you know I can't do this." Tina felt the

panic rise as her aunt pulled her into the crowd of people. "If I see him, I'll melt into a puddle."

"Don't be silly. Alexander women do not melt into puddles at men's feet." And then she added with a wink, "At least, not in public."

Walking with Yana was like the parting of the Red Sea, Tina thought. One look at how beautiful her aunt was, and people just naturally stepped aside. But tonight, Tina also felt that there were eyes on her, as well. Several of the men smiled and nodded as she passed, and the look in their eyes was clearly one of appreciation. She nodded back politely, but without interest.

There was only one man she was interested in, and he was the one man she couldn't have.

"Smile, Tina," Yana whispered. "I didn't spend the past two hours fitting this dress to you and fixing your hair for nothing. You are too stunning not to show off."

"What's the point?" Tina asked quietly. "What does it matter what I look like now? You know Reid and I can't be together. I might as well have come here wearing a sweatsuit, for all that it matters to me."

"Reid will be the one wearing a sweatsuit," Yana said with a smile. "Believe me, once he takes a look at you, he'll need a nice, long, cold shower."

"I'll be the one needing a shower," she muttered, and let her aunt lead her to the bar and order them both white wine. Since she knew she was going to have to face Reid tonight sooner or later, it just might help take the edge off her nerves.

When a hand closed around her arm, she turned.

Looks like it was going to be sooner, she thought, staring into Reid's deep-blue gaze.

"Buy you a drink?" he said softly.

Her heart was too busy doing somersaults to listen to her brain telling her not to fall into his arms. "Okay," she said, more than a little breathless at his touch.

"Don't be impressed, Katina." Yana stepped between them and gently removed Reid's hand from Tina's arm. "The drinks are free. Hello, Reid."

Without taking his eyes off Tina, Reid nodded. "Yana."

Torn between distress and relief at her aunt's interference, Tina barely managed a smile. "It's a lovely party."

"It is now." He took Tina's arm again. "Why don't I show you around?"

"I believe you've already done that, dear," Yana said firmly. "And smile for the camera, would you?"

The hard line on Reid's mouth curved into a smile, and he let go of Tina's arm at the same moment the photographer stepped in front of them. Smiling, Yana moved in closer to Reid, blocking Tina just as the flash of the camera went off. When the photographer moved on, Reid reached for Tina again.

But Yana was too quick. She slipped her arm into Reid's and smiled at him. "Why don't you take both of us on a tour?"

He glanced from Yana to Tina. "Sure."

Trying not to chew off her lipstick, Tina followed hesitantly behind her aunt and Reid. What she should do was run, but she was too weak. Too foolish.

Too much in love.

She half listened while Reid gave a brief history of Crofthaven, that it was built over a hundred years ago by his great-grandfather, Hiram Danforth, and was considered a historical landmark. The chandeliers and marble were imported from Europe, the grounds meticulously cared for by an army of gardeners. As they walked through the main entry, Tina marveled at the high ceilings and white columns, the spectacular staircase, the glossy hardwood floors and beautiful furnishings.

But mostly she marveled at the pleasure of simply being with Reid.

Pulling her gaze back to the tour, Tina followed Reid and her aunt down a hall off the main entry. They glanced into the music room, which held an elegant baby grand, then moved on to the library. The floor-to-ceiling shelves were mahogany, he explained, the books an ever-growing collection of classic, contemporary and reference.

Being so close and not being able to touch him, to stand close and breathe in the familiar scent of him was driving her insane. To distract herself she moved to the opposite side of the library and examined a leather-bound collection of twentieth-century Southern poets. When she heard the click of the library door, she turned and realized that Yana had left.

Alone. She and Reid were alone.

Her hand shook as she carefully slid the book back into its place on the shelf, then turned to face him. He watched her, his gaze so intense it took her breath away.

"I've missed you," he said evenly.

She glanced away. "Reid—"

He started toward her. She took a step back.

"This isn't over." He kept moving, making her pulse skip, then race. "*We* aren't over."

If only she knew what to do with her hands, maybe she wouldn't want so badly to reach out to him, to tell him she missed him, too, that she didn't want it to be over. All she could do was shake her head.

"I've made a decision, Tina."

He never once took his eyes off her, just kept coming. This time when she moved away from him, she ended up in a corner. With nowhere to go, she pressed her back to the shelves and held her breath.

"Tina." He said her name again so softly, so longingly, she wanted to cry. "I love you."

Her breath shuddered from her lungs. Had she heard him right? "You...you love me?"

"Yes."

When he touched her cheek, she closed her eyes, knew she was trembling, but couldn't stop. How was it possible to feel so wonderful, when she felt so awful at the same time?

Dear God, help me. For this one moment she couldn't lie, couldn't hold back. Just this one moment.

"I love you, too."

"Good." He moved in so close his thighs were touching hers. "It helps when people get married if they love each other."

Married! Her eyes flew open. He wanted to marry her?

Her heart soared, then immediately took a nosedive

and she looked away. "You know that's not possible."

"I won't be without you." He tucked a finger under her chin and brought her face back to his, gazed down at her with a determination that almost had her hoping, almost had her believing. "I can't be without you," he added softly.

"Nothing has changed," she said, struggling against the moisture burning her eyes.

"Then *we'll* make the change. We'll go to Europe." He placed a hand on the wall on either side of her head and leaned in. "It would take months for anyone to track us down there, if ever. We'll live in a villa off the coast of Spain. It's beautiful there. Let me take you. Let me marry you." His mouth brushed hers. "Let me love you."

How wonderful it sounded. She felt herself sway against him, felt her lips soften against his.

Then she pulled back, shook her head.

"How long could we be happy like that?" she said, even as she pictured how beautiful it would be. "How long before you resented me or we missed our lives here?"

She slipped under his arm, wasn't certain that her knees would carry her to the door. "I'm sorry, Reid. I want to marry you, more than you can imagine. But not like this."

At the sound of a deep voice clearing his throat, Tina spun around, gasped when she saw Abraham Danforth and her parents standing in the doorway.

"Dad." Jaw tight, Reid looked at his father, then

Mariska and Ivan. "Mariska, Ivan. Would you excuse us, please?"

They all looked at each other, then stepped into the room. Abraham closed the door behind them.

"I'm afraid this concerns all of us, son." Abraham locked the door. "We simply can't let this happen."

"For God's sake, Dad." Reid blew out a breath, then shook his head. "I love this woman. I want to marry her. I'm *going* to marry her, dammit."

"How romantic." Tears in her eyes, Mariska stepped to Tina and cupped her face in her hands. "So strong, he is. What fine children you will have."

"Mom, Dad, Mr. Danforth, I know that you all—" Tina snapped her gaze back to her mother. "What did you say?"

"I said what fine children you will have, *edes szivemn,*" Mariska repeated, this time adding the endearment. "We did not come to tell you that we object, but to give our blessing."

"But, Dad—" She looked at her father, then at Abraham. "I can't, we can't…"

"Did you really think I would stand by and do nothing?" Ivan said with as much irritation in his voice as love. "That I would let you sacrifice yourself for me?"

With the way her head was spinning, she couldn't think at all. "Everyone gets hurt," she insisted. "Our family, the Danforths. How can Reid and I—" she looked at him, felt her throat thicken with tears "—how could we possibly have any kind of happiness if we've hurt the people we love?"

"And what kind of happiness could *we* have—" Mariska said, shaking her head "—if we stole yours?"

When Reid stepped beside her and slipped an arm around her, Tina let herself lean into him, wondered how she could ever leave the safety and strength she felt there.

But they were still caught in a vicious circle, and she saw no escape.

"It did seem like quite the challenge when Ivan and Mariska called me this morning," Abraham said, moving into the room. "Until I learned one interesting bit of information. Does the name Maximilian strike a cord?"

Not to Tina it didn't, but from the expression on Reid's face, the name meant something to him.

"Johann Maximilian?" Reid asked.

Abraham glanced at Tina. "Johann Maximilian is one of our largest shipping clients in Austria. I've known the man for twenty years."

"I handle his accounts," Reid explained to Tina, though clearly he was as confused as she was by the direction of the conversation. "I've been talking with his office almost every day for over a week, trying to straighten out a mistake with a docking number."

"Which Johann was very apologetic about when I spoke with him a little while ago," Abraham said.

"I don't understand." Tina desperately wished someone would get to the point. "What does this man have to do with any of this?"

"My mother was a Maximilian before she married my father," Mariska said. "Johann is my cousin."

"You—we—have other family, too?" Tina asked. "Other than your father?"

Mariska nodded. "We left our past behind us, so that we could have a future."

"But what does all this have to do with Wilheim?" Reid asked.

"My father was always an unhappy man," Mariska said sadly. "From what I have been told by my family, when my father married my mother and went to work at Castle Marcel, he became obsessed with his own importance. He was a tyrant, in his work and at home. This I know from my own life. He kept my mother and me separated from friends and family, but he also used her family name to elevate his own reputation. When my mother died, he cut all ties to the Maximilians but still retained his status in our town. He was so furious with me when I wanted to marry your father that he would have done anything to stop me."

"So we left." Ivan stepped beside Mariska and took her hand. "Once we were settled in America, we contacted Yana. She came to the states two years later and took the name Alexander, as well. I am not proud that I did not face Wilheim," he said, looking at his wife, "but I did what I needed to do for my Mariska."

Tina put her hand to her chest, struggling to absorb everything she'd just heard. There were too many emotions coming at her at once, and her head literally reeled. Only the strong pair of arms wrapped around her kept her knees from giving out.

She glanced at Reid, then her parents and Abraham. "And now?" she asked carefully. "What now?"

"Now nothing." Abraham shrugged. "If anyone

should happen to discover that Ivan Alexander was once Ivan Savar, the records will show a clerical error. A thirty-year-old arrest warrant no longer is in force, and there is no record of any complaint ever filed." Abraham smiled. "Johann is a very thorough man."

"I talked to Johann this morning," Mariska said. "He will make sure that no one listens to the incoherent ramblings of an old man."

Still holding on to Tina with one arm, Reid held his other hand out to his father. "Thank you."

When he shook his father's hand, Reid felt something pass between them, an awareness of each other that he'd never felt before. An understanding that they faced each other man to man, not just father to son. Strange that it had taken thirty-two years to come to this moment and this place. It felt good, he realized.

It felt right.

Just as it felt right to be here with Tina at his side, and even Ivan and Mariska. He turned to Tina's parents and offered his hand to Ivan. "Sir."

Ivan's grip was like a bear's, filled with emotion. Blinking back the moisture in her eyes, Mariska leaned forward and kissed Reid's cheek. "I wish you all the happiness that my Ivan and I have shared." Dabbing at her tears, she kissed Tina, then stepped back. "My baby," she mumbled, then turned and hurried from the room.

Abraham turned to Ivan. "I have a full bottle of Palinka on ice. Would you care to join me?"

"How could I refuse such an offer?" Ivan bowed and gestured for Abraham to go first.

And then, once again, they were wonderfully, bliss-fully alone.

Reid turned Tina in his arms and gazed down at her. "You okay?"

"I…I think so." Then she smiled slowly. "Yes, I am. Better than okay, I'd say. More like wonderful."

Smiling back at her, he lowered his mouth to hers, kissed her lightly. "Do you know that I fell in love with you before I even met you?"

Surprise widened her eyes. "Before you met me?"

"Yep." He brushed his lips against hers again. "I was standing outside your office door at the bakery and I heard your voice. And then, when you turned me down for a job, well, that cinched it."

"So are you saying—" her hands slid to his chest and she ran a fingertip along the edge of his tie "—that I have to turn you down to keep your inter-est?"

"Too late for that, sweetheart." He grinned at her. "I've got you now, and I'm not letting go."

He kissed her again. Long and deep. A kiss of promise and love. When he finally lifted his head, they were both breathing hard.

"Will you marry me?" He brought her hand to his mouth and kissed her fingertips. "Our parents are ex-pecting it, you know. You have to say yes."

"I suppose we shouldn't disappoint them, should we?" she murmured. "They did go to quite a bit of trouble."

"Yes, they did." He nibbled on her wrist now, couldn't wait to get her alone and nibble on other areas. "I think we should invite Johann to the wedding, too."

"Absolutely." She drew in a breath when he touched his tongue to the pulse at her wrist. "I love you, Reid. I don't know how I would have ever lived without you."

"I wouldn't have let you." He lifted his head and smiled down at her. "Please don't make me wait too long, sweetheart. I want to give you my name, make love to you every night, wake up beside you every morning."

"I don't want to wait, either," she said softly. "It's just all so overwhelming. To think I have family I never knew. And now Rachel is married and expecting a baby, too. Sophia will never forgive me."

He furrowed his brow. "For getting married?"

"For making her the last one. With Rachel and me both married, our mother will completely and whole-heartedly focus on Sophia now."

Chuckling, Reid pulled Tina close again. "I want you to have your restaurant, too," he said. "When the campaign is over and the headquarters are shut down, I'll help you any way I can."

"That's a year away." She slid her arms around his neck. "It seems like a lifetime."

"A lifetime is what we're going to have, sweet-heart. Babies. A home. Grandbabies, great-grandbabies. That's a lifetime. God, how I love you, Katina Alexander."

"And I love you, Reid Danforth."

He leaned down to press his mouth to hers; she reached up. The kiss was sweet. Tender.

Timeless.

"What do you say we go announce it now?" he said when he finally lifted his head. "While the press is here. They're gonna love having the scoop on this one."

"The press?" She bit her lip. "Now?"

"Better get used to it, darling," he said with a grin. "You're going to be a Danforth."

"That," she said, smiling back as she pressed her mouth to his, "I can get used to."

*   *   *   *   *

Look out for Sophia's story in Barbara McCauley's contribution to a special anthology,

Dynasties: Summer in Savannah,

available this June from Silhouette Books.